Every Witch Way but Feral

Magical Misfits Mysteries - book 8

K.E. O'Connor

K.E. O'Connor Books

Chapter 1

Something's missing

I glanced over my shoulder as I ran, shaking my head as I reviewed the disastrous results of my latest spell. Getting back more of my demigoddess magic was supposed to make my life easier. But this felt the opposite of easy.

What had gone wrong?

Where was my beautiful white tail?

I'd only been playing with my power, giving it a gentle warm up, before letting it loose. I hadn't asked for that warm up to whip through me like a witch's broom and remove my glorious swish stick.

I needed help. I'd been casting spells for over an hour to get my tail to come back, and as a result, my magic battery sat on the red line.

I didn't dare disturb Zandra from her slumber and tell her what I'd done. That would only lead to lots of questions, and she was always grumpy when awoken in the middle of the night with a dilemma to unpick.

Before a hateful goblin had transformed me into a cat, I'd had no idea how much I'd value a tail. And now it was missing! And I'd been the one to remove it! I just didn't know how or what I could do to get it back.

I glanced around as I ran, grateful for the late hour, so no one would see me dashing through the streets with my invisible tail between my legs. Such a humiliation.

What I needed was answers and no judgment. And assistance. I had to get my tail back before sunup, or questions would be asked. And I had no answers to give. Well, no answers I was prepared to give. One question would lead to another and then another, and before I knew it, everything would be out in the open. And that would lead to problems. I had enough of those.

My furry friend, Sage, always said never to keep secrets because they always came and bit you on the behind. But there were some secrets that needed careful management. And those were the ones I had to keep from my wonderful witch. For now. Maybe forever. I'd yet to decide.

I paused at the large, black wrought-iron gate blocking the entrance to Remus's mansion in Oak Park Ridge. I wasn't surprised to see the place lit up, since a hive of vampires lived there, but the ramshackle tents and canvas dwellings set a short distance from the gates were unexpected. Surely, if Remus had guests, he wouldn't put them up in something so basic. Remus loved luxury and shared freely. And from the looks of those tents, most of them had seen better days. I could smell the damp from twenty feet away.

"Juno! Is that you hiding out there?" My most wonderful fuzzy hellhound friend, Archie, bounded into view, his tail wagging and his tongue hanging out one side of his enormous jaws. Jaws that could crack a skull. Although he rarely needed to use them for such a gory purpose, since just the sight of him inspired toe curling fear.

"Hush. I don't want anyone to know I'm here. Not when I look like this." I remained crouched, scouting the surroundings to make sure we weren't drawing attention.

"Oh! You're good. Everyone's inside. We've got the grounds to ourselves. Come in." Archie nudged open one of the large gates with his fuzzy muzzle and swiped his tongue across my head.

I almost avoided the tongue bath, but still got a little soggy.

"Wow! You weren't kidding about your tail. It's totally gone." He sniffed my rear end and got a swipe to the nose for his trouble.

"Why would I joke about something so important?" I felt the urge to swish my tail, but of course, it wasn't there to swish.

"You said a spell did this to you?"

I gestured with my head for him to follow me, and Archie willingly obliged. He was such an agreeable hellhound. Once we were far from the unexpected tents and the main house, I settled on the damp grass. My front paws felt naked because I was unable to wrap my tail around them. Archie joined me, his head cocked as he waited to hear the story of the stolen tail.

I settled myself some more, uncertain how to begin. "I found another piece of my missing magic. I've been experimenting with it."

"That's amazing! Where'd you get it? Was it buried like the magic I found for you? Oh! It didn't explode and blow off your tail, did it?"

"No. It was a gift. Do you recall the visit from Acer's family?"

"Sure. Her dad was killed in the park. Everyone was talking about it."

"He was. And he was a magic finder, and could retrieve anything lost. I'd asked him to help me find my missing magic, but he deceived me. Acer ensured I got back what I was entitled to."

Archie twisted his head from side to side, making his ears flap. "So, you used your magic to get rid of your tail? Why? Are you trying out a new look? Some cats never grow a tail. I've seen pictures. Weird. Cute, but weird. They must have super cold butts."

I hissed softly at him. "Absolutely not. I want my tail back. I've tried everything, but nothing works." I flopped onto my belly and heaved out a sigh of frustration and exhaustion.

"I can help. Let me. Remus has a huge cabinet of old potions and spell books. He collects them. Most of them smell funny, though."

I lifted my head. "I'd hoped there'd be something in that enormous house to help me with my situation." Having been inside Remus's home on more than one occasion, I knew he was a vampire of refined, if not sometimes over the top, taste. I'd also spotted a number of curios with a magical tang when I'd poked them with a paw.

"There will be. That cabinet stinks of old magic. Some of it even stinks like you."

I bared my teeth at him. "How do I stink?"

Archie backed away a step and lowered his head. "Sorry! That came out wrong. You stink good. Just different to other familiars. Like old spices and smoke."

"It's not getting any better."

"No! It is. I like that smell. It makes me think of deserts and pointy mountains made of bricks."

"Pyramids?"

"Yep. Those. Good stink. Old stink. Loads of power in that smell."

I understood where Archie was coming from, and he wasn't far off about where my magic had originated.

Archie turned and looked at the house. "There must be something inside to help you get your tail back."

"I'm willing to try anything. I'd also hoped to test a few combined spells with you if you're willing to share your magic."

"Anything to help. Let's see what we can do. If your tail doesn't grow back when we combine power, we'll go inside and check the cabinet. Just be prepared for the whiff. It makes me lightheaded."

"Strange smells I can handle. A missing tail, not so much." I drew in a breath and slowly climbed to my paws. I knew I could rely on Archie to help me out of this sticky situation. I'd considered talking to

Sage, but she'd have told me it was my fault, and I had to live with the consequences.

"What do you need me to do?" Archie said.

"If you have any salmon, I could do with a refuel before we begin," I said. "That fine fish has been lacking in Crimson Cove since Sorcha's café became plant based. Fish is brain food! I'm sure I'm undernourished in omega oils, which is why my magic is misfiring."

Archie scratched behind his ear with one large back paw. "We're not big fish fans here. Steak, now you're talking. Will that do? We have a freezer full of the stuff. And plenty in the kitchen ready to chew on."

"You get the food, and I'll review the spell options."

Ten minutes later, we'd both consumed a delicious hunk of steak. I was feeling better, and we were ready to cast our first spell. We'd relocated to a quiet spot in the grounds, hidden in the shadows of a grove of ancient red maples so we wouldn't be disturbed.

"How does our connection feel?" I asked Archie.

"Feeling good. All tingly. Like a tiny fairy is tapdancing along my spine and occasionally poking me in the ribs."

I tried not to dwell on the swirl of jealousy in the pit of my stomach as he wagged his glorious tail. "Let's get started." I pressed a paw on the small scroll I'd borrowed from Vorana's bookstore, twitched my ears three times, and blew across the words, sending the intention of the spell into the air and surrounding me. The magic swirled off the pages and enveloped me in a chilly breeze that pressed against my skin.

I inspected my tail. Still missing. Not even a tingly suggestion that it wanted to return. I tried the spell again, but got the same lackluster response.

"It's not working," Archie said.

"I can see that. I have others. Let's try something else."

The five other spells we tried produced the same outcome. The magic reared, but failed to materialize my tail. Was I to be a tailless cat for the rest of my life? There was a breed of cats who never grew a tail, but how did they communicate their desires without a beautiful, fluffy emotion stick attached to the base of their spine?

"We should take a break." I rolled the scroll of disappointing magic and shoved it into the small pack I carried on my back, so I could return it safely to Vorana's store before she knew I'd borrowed it.

"I can keep going. I've got loads of energy. Remus is always telling me I need at least four long walks a day, so I'm not twitchy." Archie bounced on his paws.

"I can't. I've been working on this for ages and I'm exhausted. If only I had half your energy." I flopped onto my belly and stared at a tiny black beetle as it made its way purposefully through the blades of grass.

Archie huffed a smoky breath over my head. "We'll find the solution inside the magic cabinet. I took a look while I was waiting for the steaks to heat. Everything is labeled. And the poisonous stuff is marked, so I don't think anything will kill you."

"Comforting thought." I dragged my paws as I followed Archie to a low door at the back of the mansion.

Remus was an indulgent hellhound owner, and had installed automatic doors in certain sections of the walls for Archie to use, so he could get in and out anytime of the day and night without disturbing the vampires.

He pressed his nose against the door, and it opened smoothly, allowing us inside. It was only a short trot before we entered an opulently decorated hallway, lined with original oil paintings of various influential vampires, and a flooring so soft it made me want to pause and make biscuits with my paws.

I slowed at the sound of raised voices, although the tone was more amused than angry. "I meant to ask, does Remus have guests? I saw the tents outside."

"More like intruders. This way." Archie led me past a closed door, where the excitable voices could be heard, and into a room that looked like a museum exhibit from Victorian England. There were a dozen glass curiosity cabinets lining the walls. Each one was full of different colored bottles, crumbling leather-bound books, and even a few framed scrolls containing excerpts from magic spells.

I took my time to inspect each one. "I never realized Remus had access to so much magic. Why does he collect spells when he's a vampire?"

"Because I have a curiosity about life and power, you charming bundle of inquisitive fluff."

Remus Salamander stepped into the room, dressed immaculately in a soft cream suit with a matching waistcoat and top hat covering his shoulder-length blond hair.

"I'm helping Juno. Look at her tail!" Archie bounded over and got a hearty head scratch from his adoring vampire companion.

"I'm trying to, but it appears to be missing." One corner of Remus's mouth lifted. "Is that why you're inspecting my curiosity room? You think your tail may be a new exhibit?"

I gave him a hard stare. "I'd better not find my missing tail in here, or we'll have words."

Remus chuckled as he wandered into the room. "Fear not, Juno. I have far too much respect for you to steal something so valuable. But I'm fascinated to learn where your tail has gone. Do tell the story."

Archie opened his mouth to explain, but a sharp look from me had him clamping his jaw shut, and a gentle whimper slid out.

"Merely a spell gone wrong. I've been trying various ways to return my tail, but since it's being so elusive, I decided I needed a little assistance," I said.

"And of course, you knew Archie would oblige." Remus's tone was light, but there was an edge of steel to his words. He allowed no one to exploit Archie.

"We're friends. Friends help each other."

"And I want to help. Juno looks weird without a tail. I mean, still nice, but weird. Like a plump white badger," Archie said.

I hissed at him. "I am not plump!"

"It's the giant portions Vorana feeds you. She's always shown her love through food." Remus strode around me as he stroked his chin, a thoughtful yet playful look on his face. "How about feathers? You could fashion a beautiful, unique tail with feathers. You'd be the talk of the town."

"For the wrong reason," I grumbled. "I want my actual tail back."

"We could fashion you a delightful false tail." Remus glanced around the room. "Clive is handy. He's into woodworking. How would a wooden tail suit you?"

I ignored him as I strutted around, inspecting the contents of the different cabinets, still looking for a solution to my missing tail.

"That's a no to a wooden tail? You're right. It wouldn't be comfortable or warm. Although, we could clad it in something soft. What do you think, Archie?"

"I think you're teasing Juno, and she's getting grumpy." Archie raised a paw and whined. He hated confrontation, no matter how mild.

"Perhaps, a little." Remus bowed his head. "Apologies, Juno. It has been a stressful evening, so I'm glad of a diversion to let off steam. May I make a suggestion?"

"So long as it involves nothing made of wood that gets attached to my rear end," I said.

"Wear your lack of tail with pride. You're a stunning cat, and one that comes with great power. Others respect you, and they look up to you. You may even start a trend."

I snorted my disbelief. "You think other familiars will magic away their tails because I was foolish enough to do so to myself?"

"I've heard of more curious occurrences." Remus tilted back his head. "I remember the trend for ultra-pointy shoes after the king was seen wearing a pair. And don't get me started on Hennin hats, bombast sleeves, and bliauts."

"Which king was this?"

"One of the Henry's. It was such a long time ago. How about—"

"I'll figure things out. I just need to get used to my new..." I hesitated. I'd almost given the game away that my old magic had done this to me.

Remus arched an eyebrow. "Yes? Your new what?"

I waved a paw in the air. "It's nothing. My mistake, my fix."

He pursed his lips, not happy with my explanation. "You may look around my curiosity cabinets, but most of the magic is past its prime and unstable. You may lose a limb or an ear if you go throwing it around."

"It could still be useful." I eyed a beautiful jeweled wooden box with gold edging.

"All antiques. Collectables, rather than solutions to magical problems." Remus froze, then his eyes narrowed and his fangs flashed into view. A second later, raised voices sounded outside, and they had no hint of cheer to them.

"If you'll excuse me. My persistent problem is causing difficulties." He turned and strode to the door, Archie on his heels.

"Problems?" I dashed after them. "You mean your tent dwellers?"

"Environmental protesters." Remus hurried along the corridor to the main door. "Their leader, Gaian Scythe, has decided they're to disrupt our plans for the Blood Moon Festival."

"Sorcha's new carrot loving boyfriend is causing you trouble?"

"He's been an unwelcome thorn in my side since he arrived in Crimson Cove after having swept the delectable Sorcha off of her sensible shoes. And when he learned about our plans to celebrate the Blood Moon, he made it his mission to disrupt our fun."

"Gaian sent the people in the tents?" I asked.

Remus yanked open the front door and strode out ahead of us. "He did. Excuse me. I must ensure no-one's neck gets snapped. My hive is protective of their home. We will not tolerate intruders."

"The vampires are furious about what's happening." Archie stopped walking, his focus on Remus and his gaze anxious. "They've been looking forward to the Blood Moon Festival all year. It's the most important vampire festival on the calendar."

"What are Gaian's friends protesting about?" I stayed with Archie as Remus joined several of his smartly dressed hive vampires, and they headed to the tents, where a group of scruffy, grumpy looking individuals stood. Most of them had beards.

"All of it! But especially the hog roasts."

I glanced up at him. "Not the twelve individuals who'll be drained on the night?"

"Not so much. After all, vampires must eat. And anyone who gets drained has consented to being part of the event. They all want to be turned. That's the deal. Blood donation for a chance to join the hive. No one refuses an offer like that."

I shook my head. "These plant loving protesters are more interested in protecting pigs than people!"

"They're weird. And Remus is unhappy. I've never seen him so mad. They're also stubborn. Nothing is getting them to move on. And they need to leave soon because the fun begins after the next moon fall."

"I've met Gaian a few times. He is dedicated to his cause. And he seems dedicated to Sorcha. She's even moved him in."

"I heard." Archie wrinkled his massive muzzle. "He has those snappy hounds that follow him around. I don't like them. I went to say hello, and they jumped on me!"

"They weren't friendly to me, either. I've felt like something has been stalking ever since they arrived. And I don't know if you've been to the café recently, but most of the menu is now plant based." That sad news earned a shake of my head. "No salmon for me. I used to love Sorcha's smoked salmon. It was melt in the mouth."

Archie whined and ducked his head, so he was eye level with me. "Bad times, Juno. No fish and no tail!"

I huffed out a breath. "I'll fix all of this. Will Remus cancel the festival if the protesters keep being difficult?"

"No chance. You're still coming, aren't you? You and Zandra must come. It'll be amazing."

"Of course. Wouldn't miss it, especially not if there are troublemakers that need watching."

"Good. I want all of my friends here." Archie lowered his ears. "I'm glad you came by before everything got busy. I've been meaning to talk to you about something."

I narrowed my gaze as a protestor waved a homemade banner. "What's that?"

"Don't get angry, but I've been asking around about Sammy. I miss that little guy, and I was hoping if I reached out and invited him to the Blood Moon Festival, we could clear the air and fix the troubles with Angel Force."

My heart sank to my toe beans. "That's good of you, but Sammy's been gone a long time. He could be anywhere." Or nowhere, if he hadn't thrived on his own, injured and friendless.

"He always loved a party. Sure, it was tough to get him on the dancefloor, but once he got into the groove, Sammy always had a great time. Crimson Cove doesn't feel the same without him here."

"I miss him, too. And I know, for all the trouble Tinkerbell caused Sorcha, she misses her as well."

"I'll keep asking around. Maybe someone's seen them together, and they can let them know they're missed. They can't have vanished."

I looked at my missing tail. "Where magic is concerned, anything is possible." I stood, stretched, and rubbed my face against Archie's. "I'd better get home to Zandra. I'll see you later at the festival. Hopefully, with my tail back where it belongs."

Chapter 2

Protestor problems

"Are you sure you don't know what happened to your tail?" My wonderful witch, Zandra Crypt, hoisted an empty animal pen into the back of the work van and then closed and locked the door. "Where'd it go?"

Unfortunately, my plans to restore my tail before Zandra woke had hit a snag. The snag being, no matter what spell I used, my tail was determined not to show itself.

"I wish I could explain it to you. But this is the situation. It simply vanished overnight."

"Hmmm... you're fudging the truth." Zandra turned and crossed her arms over her chest, decked out in her usual practical T-shirt, jeans, and stomping boots. "There's more to the story than you simply woke and your tail was no longer there."

"It's this town! It's full of powerful magic that spills over. My missing tail is the result of such a spillage. I'm working on getting it back. It's a temporary loss."

"Uh-huh. More like, you messed with a spell that was too big for your paws, and this is the result."

She crouched and scratched me under my chin. "Did you poke around in the magic chest? I don't mind. Adrienne gifted it to me, but there's more than enough to share. What did you use? One of the firestone amulets? I can never get those things to do anything."

"No, it's not that. I didn't go near your chest."

One of her eyebrows rose. "Tails don't just disappear."

"How do you know? Do you have one?"

She smirked. "It must feel weird not to have it."

"It does. I feel naked. Perhaps I'm part lizard, though, and I've only just found out." After all, I hadn't always been a cat. Maybe there was more to the spell that kept me trapped in this form than I realized. Could I be evolving?

It was a tiny thread of possibility to cling to, but I was almost certain my magic had done this to me.

"More like part secret keeper. You don't need to keep things from me. I'm a big girl," Zandra said.

I twitched my booping snooter. That was part of the problem. As wonderful as my witch was, she'd messed with serious magic when she was a child. It meant she'd grown up faster than she should have done and missed many formative years.

When I'd joined her as her familiar, I realized she needed protecting. Not just from other magic users, but from herself. Zandra needed to catch up on the things she'd missed.

It was a big part of why I didn't tell her everything about my past. I wasn't certain she'd be able to handle it. Even if she did, what's to say she'd accept her familiar was more than meets the eye?

Zandra gave me one more chin scratch. "I'll help you find your tail. If we have to, we could even spend the evening in Vorana's bookstore, browsing the shelves. Maybe there's a spell to find a lost tail."

That showed true devotion, since Zandra and books weren't best friends. "I've already looked. I was there for hours last night."

"When? We spent the evening together."

"After you went to sleep. I didn't want to disturb you, but I couldn't sleep when I realized my tail had gone, so went to see what I could learn."

Zandra rolled her eyes, then stood. "You worry about me too much. We're here to help each other. And I can handle some lost sleep."

"We do help each other. I was a marvelous help today, dealing with that bewitched crow when it almost took your head off."

"So, I'll return the favor. I'll dig around and find something that'll regrow your tail." Zandra went to run a hand over the stump, but I inched away, and she drew back. "Sorry! Does it hurt when I touch you?"

"No, but it feels odd when anything brushes against my... stump." I glanced at my oddly bare rear end. "I know what should be there, but there's nothing. I feel its absence. And my balance is less than perfect. I didn't realize how much I relied upon my fluff poll to stop me from falling."

"If you fall, I'll catch you. Every time."

I rested my front paws on Zandra's knee, and we gently touched foreheads. "I know you will. And I'll do the same for you. We can search for a solution to my missing tail together. But first, I need to tell you about Remus."

We'd been so busy at animal control during the day that we'd barely had time to eat and take comfort breaks, let alone gossip about the Blood Moon Festival.

"Something good? They must be busy getting ready. Are we still planning on going tonight?"

"Wouldn't miss it."

Zandra wrinkled her nose. "We could wait until Sunday. It'll be less crowded."

She wasn't a fan of noisy parties, and I often had to chivvy her out of the basement apartment we rented from Vorana, or she'd become a full-time hermit with a dozen cat companions. And I didn't share my witch.

I shook my head. "I've been asking around, and the first night is always the best."

"And the busiest." Zandra grimaced.

"Remus will want us there. Especially since he's having problems."

Zandra stood and stretched her arms over her head. "What are we talking about? Have his wannabe vampires changed their minds? He'll have no trouble getting replacements. For some weird reason, there's always a queue of willing victims wanting to be sucked dry by the undead."

"It's not a problem with his willing victims. It's Sorcha's boyfriend. Gaian's set protesters on Remus. And when I visited Archie last night, they were arguing with the vampires."

"That's where you got to. I woke, and you were gone. I figured you'd gone upstairs for a midnight snack with Sage, but I didn't hear you come back."

"I went to spend time with Archie and discuss my tail issues. I thought he'd help. But that's beside the point. Gaian and his protestors want the Blood Moon Festival canceled."

"He doesn't think the vampires should feed?"

"Gaian is protesting because there'll be hog roasts."

Zandra groaned. "Let me guess, he wants carrot hot dogs and tofu burgers in their place? Imagine what the vampires would think about that for their guests?"

"It would be a bloodbath. The vampires have a right to celebrate their origins and give thanks for the power they've been given. Just the same as the werewolves."

"And the witches. Think of the carnage that would unfurl if Gaian and his protesters showed up at any of our events?"

I chuckled. "He'd be frazzled. Or blown apart. Or shrunk into a poppet and have pins stuck in him by all the angry witches."

Zandra huffed a laugh. "Which is why he's going after the vampires. At least their methods of attack are more obvious."

"Unless they change into bat form and swoop him? Or smoke and smother him in his sleep."

"Don't let Sorcha hear you talk like that. They've become inseparable." Zandra rested her hands on her hips. "I still can't believe she's moved him in. They've only been together a few months.

That's too soon to co-habit. Too soon to even be exclusive."

"When the heart knows..."

"Sorcha's heart needs serious investigation if she thinks that guy's the perfect one for her. Although, those roasted tofu steaks she serves with the crispy fries and siracha sauce are tasty."

"It's no match for a good old-fashioned smoked salmon and cream cheese bagel," I said.

Zandra lifted a hand. "You'll get no arguments from me. At least Sorcha is still making her banana pancakes."

I twitched my whiskers. "When the café is open."

She rubbed the back of her neck. "Yeah, it's becoming a problem. You'd think they'd be out of the honeymoon phase by now and things would be getting stale. Sorcha should focus on the café and not on making her guy happy."

"Does that mean it's true love?"

Zandra poked out her tongue. "If this is true love, then leave me out. And Vorana is heartbroken since Sorcha dumped her. They've barely seen each other since Gaian rocked up with his swagger and planty ideas."

I nodded as we strolled away from the van and headed toward town, our work done for the day. This was the first time either of us had seen Sorcha Creer in love. And, although she was physically glowing, she scored zero points for being a decent friend. She'd abandoned us in a heartbeat. And she'd been friends with Vorana for years before we'd moved to Crimson Cove, and Vorana had barely heard from Sorcha in weeks. Although

Vorana put on a brave face, it wounded her to be so swiftly dumped.

"Where should we go for dinner before we head to the festival?" I said. "Home or away?"

"We're going to the café. Sorcha held out an olive branch today. She sent a message and asked me to meet her there after work."

"Maybe she's tiring of the environmentalists and wants to tag along with us and avoid the protests. She must feel embarrassed by Gaian. Sure, he's gorgeous and has a list of admirable values he lives by, salmon shaming excluded, but he's interfering in something he shouldn't." I nodded my approval. "Sorcha is finally distancing herself from him."

"I wondered if there was trouble in paradise. And it'll be good to touch base and smooth things over. I hated how we left things the last time we spoke."

I was glad to learn Sorcha had reached out. Things had been tense between them since they'd argued, and Zandra questioned whether Gaian was responsible for leaving the strange symbols around town.

"Sorcha should be involved with the Blood Moon Festival," I said. "After all, she's more vampire than anything else. She needs to celebrate the wonderful power that runs through her veins."

"She should. And if we can get her away from Gaian for more than five minutes, I want to talk to her about him."

I flicked an ear. "You think he's keeping her from us?"

Zandra lifted her shoulders. "I have no clue. And I won't until I get her on her own and make sure he's not one of those creepy guys who cuts his girl off from friends and loved ones."

"Then let's get her to the Blood Moon Festival tonight. Agreed?"

Zandra sighed. "Agreed."

As we approached Sorcha's café, it was clear we weren't the only ones who'd been invited. There was no space inside the café, and music drifted out, along with laughter and the now familiar scent of fried tofu. A group of thirty people milled around outside, chatting and chilling. They were dressed to impress in colorful mini dresses, tie dye shirts with sparkled edges, and flappy shorts.

A pretty blonde woman in her late twenties wearing a tiny pair of denim shorts and a bejeweled bra encasing an impressively bouncy bust, bray-laughed as she stroked her hand down an attractive dark-haired guy's arm. He flashed her a smile, his blue eyes rimmed with guyliner, and wrapped an arm around her tiny waist.

Several other guys lurking close by watched her, looking as if they wanted to be the one to wrap their arms around her waist and whisper sweet nothings in her ear.

"Briar's showing off again." A stout, mousy woman in her late twenties with round glasses and wearing an oversized flowered cotton poncho nudged her friend.

The friend shrugged. "We knew she'd be like this. It's typical Briar behavior. She'll get bored soon enough and move on to the next conquest. There's too much temptation here for her to stick with one guy all weekend."

"And I'll be left to pick up the pieces, as usual. You two are irresponsible. I should never have agreed to this trip." The stout woman gripped her poncho, bunching it in her fist, before striding toward the café and pushing inside.

Her abandoned friend rolled her eyes, then took a sip from a bottle of cider.

"Magic brownie?" An elderly woman with deep set wrinkles around her mouth and a hunched back stepped in front of us and held out a tray of delicious looking chocolate chip brownies. "Make you float."

Zandra inspected the tray. "They look amazing. What's in them?"

"All perfectly legal. My goodies have been inspected and taste tested by Angel Force. They enjoyed them so much, I suggested they put them on the lunch menu to help those beautiful creatures fly without flapping their wings." The woman chuckled.

I hopped onto Zandra's shoulder. "You're supplying brownies for Sorcha's café?"

"No, cutie pie. I have a brownie stand at the festival. I'll be supplying delicious treats for the hard workers."

"The workers being the protestors?"

"Anyone who wants them. But these poor creatures will have a difficult job tackling the vampires, so they'll need plenty of chocolaty fuel to keep them going."

My gaze flickered over the noisy crowd. "Everyone here is planning on protesting at the Blood Moon Festival?"

"Yes! They're calling themselves the rear guard." She leaned closer. "I heard a team camped at the festival last night to get the lay of the land. Is that what you're here for? First time protesters?"

"Something like that." Zandra looked unimpressed at this alarming news. Remus would be furious that his event was about to be hijacked by even more protestors. Add this group to the ones already there, and he'd have over a hundred troublemakers on his manicured hands.

"If you have any questions about what to do, just ask for Edith. That's me. Edith Emory's Enchanting Eats. I've been coming to these events for decades, so I know what to look out for and when to duck when things get intense." She held out the tray and speared a brownie. "Are you sure I can't tempt you? They take the edge off. Make you nice and chilled."

"We're good. Thanks," I said. "Is Sorcha around?"

"That's the lady who owns the café?"

I nodded.

"She's inside. They're making the final preparations before the big off. We're walking to the festival. Although, I've already got my stand set up, ready for customers. I set up as soon as I arrived, since I was late getting here." She rested a hand on the small of her back and stretched. "It's hard work selling treats."

"Hey! Don't be rude. And keep your hands off of what you can't afford." The pretty blonde in the tiny shorts stepped away from a guy with a black beard almost to his waist and a mean glint in his eyes.

He stepped closer, and she shoved him in the chest.

"Oh, dear. That's the kind of trouble I keep an eye on. All these pretty girls in their sparkles, and the lusty young men who overstep their boundaries. I'm like an old mother hen. I always make sure the young ones don't get in over their heads." Edith bustled away and maneuvered herself in between the blonde and the guy and calmed the situation, sending the guy in one direction with a brownie and the blonde stomping away.

"Gaian's been busy making Remus's life difficult," Zandra muttered as she inched her way through the crowd, getting closer to the café entrance.

"And Remus won't be happy with more unwanted guests showing up and messing with his festival," I said.

"There you are!" Sorcha detached herself from Gaian's lap the second we were inside and pushed through the throng of bodies to meet us. "I wasn't sure you'd show."

"I got your message. And I said we'd be here." Zandra tucked her hands behind her after a brief tug on the end of her hair. A sign she was nervous. "I didn't expect all these people, though."

Sorcha nodded, a grin on her face. "It's bigger than I expected, too, but Gaian said there'd be a crowd."

"You're really planning on disrupting the Blood Moon Festival?" I said.

"Of course."

"I assumed you'd want to join in. You must have been to the event in previous years, given your vampire connections."

Sorcha's smile faltered. "Sure, I've been before. But this year is different. Gaian's opened my eyes to so many things."

"Unfortunately, not how to make tofu taste like salmon," I muttered.

"Here. You'll need these." Sorcha grabbed two protest placards. One was small, with a loop of rope around it. It read: *pigs are people, too*. The other said: *stop the bloodshed*.

"You invited us here because you want us to join in with your protest?" Zandra shook her head. "I've got nothing against Remus."

"But there are alternatives to what he has planned. He doesn't have to make everything so grizzly." Sorcha shuddered.

"He's a vampire. Sometimes, things get bloody," I said. "You should know."

Sorcha's eyes narrowed. "Stop bringing up my past. People can change. I've changed."

I wrinkled my booping snooter at her sharp tone. "Are you suddenly not a vampire?"

"I didn't say that." Sorcha glanced over her shoulder. "But Gaian's opened my eyes—"

"Are you able to think for yourself anymore? Or does Gaian do all the thinking and planning for you?" Zandra's gaze flicked over Sorcha. "I see he's changed your dress sense, too."

Her mouth dropped open as she smoothed a hand over her cropped black T-shirt and tiny shorts. "Of course not. It's just that—"

"It's just that, ever since Gaian came into your life, you've been unable to have a thought for yourself. He's changed the café, changed you, got you pretending you're not part vampire, and now this." Zandra waved a hand in the air. "Remus has always been good to you. He's never hassled you because you're not in his hive. It's more than most master vamps would do. And this is how you repay him?"

I gently nipped Zandra's ear. She was right to feel frustrated, but raising her voice and pointing out Sorcha's faults wouldn't win her brownie points.

Sorcha licked her lips. "There's nothing wrong with learning new things and changing your mind."

"So long as you're changing your mind and not letting Gaian influence you." Zandra looked around the crowded café. "I should talk to him."

"No! He's busy." Sorcha folded her arms over her chest. "Does that mean you won't help us?"

Zandra copied the posture. "We're not protesting."

The two friends glared at each other, neither willing to back down.

Sorcha finally huffed out a breath. "Zandra, you must see sense. You must know what's important."

"The Blood Moon Festival has been important to vampires for thousands of years," I said. "They always celebrate it. They're not going to stop because your boyfriend doesn't like it."

"Remus will back down, eventually." Gaian appeared behind Sorcha and wrapped an arm around her shoulders. Behind him lurked the gang's three bristled furred gray hounds, their teeth bared and their focus on me.

"Why should he back down?" I kept a close watch on the hounds, in case they risked a lunge to grab me off of Zandra's shoulder. "Remus has a right to celebrate an ancient tradition that's important to the vampires."

"We're not condemning their traditions, but we're condemning the loss of life his twisted traditions cause." Gaian wore his trademark fake leather, his dark hair swept off his handsome face in a messy man bun.

"You're talking about the hog roasts, not the people that'll be turned?" I asked.

"The people make their choices freely. The hogs have no choice if they wish to take part." Gaian curled his top lip. "Although, of course, we'll make sure Remus's feast of choice wasn't pressured into their decision."

"Good luck with that," Zandra said. "Remus has a waiting list of thousands who want to join his hive. And he won't let you anywhere near them so you can interfere."

"We're already interfering. I had an advance party set up a couple of nights ago to see what he was up to."

"I've already seen your tent dwellers," I said.

"My scouts. They're reporting back hourly as to the festival's progress." Gaian's mouth lifted in a half smile. "I'm satisfied we're making Remus rethink his plans."

"Or making him think about sneaking up on you in the dead of night and draining you dry," Zandra muttered.

Sorcha tutted. "We're not here to cause problems, but Remus is out of touch with modern life. He must change."

"He won't."

Sorcha glared at Zandra. "If you're not backing us on this, you can leave."

"I will. I only came here because I thought you'd come to your senses."

"My senses are crystal clear."

A tremor of hot magic seeped out of Zandra and tingled my toe beans, and I felt her jaw move as she ground her teeth.

"Juno, I thought you'd be on our side," Gaian said smoothly. "My gang stands for the planet and the animals. Even the unique ones missing their tails."

The hounds behind him sniggered.

I drew myself to my full height and hissed, glad of my white fluff to hide the heat creeping through my body.

Gaian spread his hands in a gesture of appeasement. "We're here to make the world better, and the vampires are welcome to join us. There have been successful studies to show vampires can survive on fewer feeds."

"Survive but not thrive," I said. "Their instinct is to hunt and feast freely. If you take that away, it's as bad as declawing and removing the teeth of the finest big cat. It's cruel and unnatural."

Gaian lifted one shoulder. "Supernaturals must adapt or die. It's nature's way."

"Vampires are immortal," I murmured.

"Not if they get a stake through the heart." Although Gaian smiled, there was no warmth in his eyes.

"If you were my friend, you'd take these placards and join us." Sorcha thrust the placards at Zandra.

Zandra batted them away. "That's unfair! Of course, we're friends. Despite your lousy choice of boyfriend."

"Then help us! Or stop standing in our way."

"Take the placards," I whispered into Zandra's ear. "We need to leave and tell Remus what's coming his way."

After a second of hesitation, Zandra grabbed the placards and tucked them under her arm.

"I knew you'd see sense," Sorcha said. "I told you, didn't I, Gaian? Zandra's smart. She always does the right thing."

"You called it, babe." He kissed the top of her head. "And with a Crypt witch on our side, we'll have even more influence. Maybe you could get the rest of your family here, and we'll show those vamps what we can really do."

"They're busy," Zandra muttered, a dull flush of fury scorching her cheeks.

A rush of people pushed inside the café, making it claustrophobic and even more over-heated. The music grew louder, and we were jostled. I almost lost my grip on Zandra's shoulder and had to dig in my claws to avoid dropping onto the evil-eyed hounds and their drooling muzzles.

"We'll leave you to it." Zandra placed a hand on my side to keep me steady.

"Everyone is heading to Oak Park Ridge in half an hour," Sorcha said, her attention on Gaian. "See you there?"

"Can't wait." Zandra turned and shoved her way out of the café, using a placard to swipe stubborn people out of our path.

As soon as we were around the corner and out of sight, she dumped the protest placards into the nearest dumpster.

"I hate that guy." Zandra looked over her shoulder. "What has he done to Sorcha?"

"I wish I could tell you. Perhaps he's an incredible kisser."

She snorted a laugh. "He'd have to be a mythical lothario to enchant her. He's turned her against Remus! They've always been close. And Sorcha has always looked out for the local vampires who struggle."

"We need to warn Remus what's coming for his festival. These protestors are about to ruin his weekend. And if we're not careful, turn Crimson Cove into a bloodbath."

Chapter 3

Troubled fun

"Sorry for the last-minute call. I know your shift has ended, but I couldn't get hold of Oleander, and Glenda's on leave." Barney Hoffman signed the last of his paperwork and looked up from his desk. "I'll pay you double time for coming back in."

"It wasn't a problem. And we were close by when we got your message," Zandra said. "To be honest, you got us out of a tricky situation. Have you seen what's going on at Sorcha's café?"

"I saw how busy it was when I went out to get coffee and pastries. Is it some sort of party?"

I glanced up from the pile of papers I'd been considering sitting on. "They're planning to disrupt the Blood Moon Festival this evening."

"Disrupt it how?" Barney glanced at my rear end, but didn't comment on my lack of tail as he filed the paperwork on the three-toed pink spotted brown owl we'd been called in to capture after it got trapped in a basement and threatened to blow the place apart.

"We're unsure, but it involves placards. I expect there'll be chanting and general mischief." I nudged Zandra's arm with my head. "And I know it won't be fun, but we need to make sure Remus knows what's coming his way. A startled vampire rarely behaves well."

She sighed. "Sure. Barney, if you don't need us for anything else, we need to go."

"Of course. Go! Go. Will the angels be at the festival?" His gaze flicked to my rear again, and he cleared his throat before rising from his chair.

"Cythera won't let this pass unnoticed." Zandra stood from her seat, and we headed out of Barney's office and along the corridor.

"I expect it's been in her calendar for months, ringed and highlighted with the words *don't let the vampires have fun*," I said.

Barney bustled along behind us. "Cythera never stands for lawbreaking. If I get a chance, I'll stop by later and see what the fuss is about."

After a quick goodbye, we dashed out of the office.

"We need to hurry. The protesters could be at Remus's mansion by now," I said.

Zandra slowed her pace, and indecision wavered on her face. "I'm not sure I want to get involved. Sorcha was so angry and defensive when we talked. I might make things worse if I show up."

"Sorcha was defending her man. It clouded her senses. Lust does that."

"Which is why I'm determined to remain single. No lusting for me."

"Not even a dose of serious liking?"

"Not even that. A life of singledom and spinster memes awaits."

I had plans for Zandra's determined singledom, but now wasn't the time to discuss it. "I'll translocate us. We can see how much damage has been done by Gaian and his protestors." I hopped onto Zandra's shoulder and cast a translocation spell that landed us outside of Remus's mansion.

The tents were still up, and there were a few more protesters milling around, but other than that, it was only the food and drink stands that were busy selling to visitors eager to celebrate the Blood Moon. Most of them weren't vampires, so they must be here because they loved all things vampy. Vampires had a unique and loyal following. I blamed the movies.

There was no sign of Gaian and his fake leather clad trouble makers or their smelly bikes.

"This isn't so bad." Zandra blew out a breath. "Not too busy. And we got here in time."

The ground trembled as Archie rocketed over, almost knocking Zandra off her feet as he barged into her.

I hissed at him. "Calm yourself. And be careful around my witch. What's the matter?"

"Nothing! You should see all the hog roasts. There are so many."

"That's what's got you so excited?" I stood in front of Zandra to protect her from any more of Archie's overenthusiastic barging.

"After those stinky protesters were rude to Remus, he doubled his food order. He paid a fortune to get more hog roasts delivered. And the lobster tanks! Six of them, all full with prime lobster. There's even a pen of lambs at the back."

"I shudder to think what he'll do with them," Zandra said.

Archie wagged his tail. "It's just for show. They'll go to the sanctuary after this is over."

"Remus has a lamb sanctuary?" I'd have flicked my tail in surprise if I had one.

"Sure. Well, not one he owns. But he has contacts. And he loves animals. Me especially. He mainly gets the hog roasts for me, but I'll never eat that many. The festival goers will help eat some, though. And the roasts smell amazing. Come see."

"Do I get a lobster?" My mouth filled with saliva at the prospect of delicious, freshly caught lobster.

"You can have a tank of them if you like! They're big, though. You'll never eat a whole one on your own."

"Watch me!"

"Juno, let's focus on the protesters, not the food," Zandra murmured.

"I can do both. And you like lobster, too. We could share."

"I'm more a fried fish kind of girl. I prefer my fish in batter with a side order of fries."

Archie ran around us several times, and only a sharp paw swipe from me across his furry muzzle stopped him from knocking into Zandra again.

"Slow down! And concentrate," I said. "What else has got you so fired up?"

"Remus has doubled the number of turnings. Twenty-four new vampires will be made tonight. He said it's never been done before, but he won't let Gaian and his goons spoil the festival. Tonight is all about the vampires."

"That's risky." I drew in a breath. "If Remus turns them all, he'll have a job on his hands to keep them under control. Baby vampires are feisty." And when I say feisty, I mean vicious, out of control killing machines with no self-control and a blood lust that won't be sated.

"He must be bluffing," Zandra said. "That's a heap of work. If Remus is busy turning so many people, he won't get to have fun at his own festival."

"They won't all make it. There are casualties at every turning," I said. "It's the risk they take to gain immortality."

"The whole hive will help with the new vampires. It's all been arranged," Archie said. "And Remus can do anything he sets his mind to. He's amazing. He called the next twelve candidates on his list and they were all available to come to the festival tonight. They're already here and going through their preparations." Archie wagged his tail. "We'll show those protesters. No one spoils our Blood Moon Festival."

"That's right, my adorable bundle of fluffy perfection." Remus appeared from the shadows. He was a delicious sight, dressed head to toe in a dusky pink suit with a matching top hat and complementary handkerchief poking from the top pocket of his immaculately tailored jacket.

"Greetings, Remus. Been listening long?" I asked.

"I only listen to interesting conversations, and yours are always of the highest quality, so I can never resist a snoop." He indulged me with a smile.

"You're sure all of this is a good idea?" Zandra said. "There are more protesters on the way. It could get messy if they won't budge."

"I'm aware of that. Which is why I'm displaying my strength. I won't be disrespected in my home." Remus lifted his chin toward the red-tinted, full rising moon. "I've even extended an invitation to the local werewolves. Although they celebrate the Blood Moon differently, they appreciate what we stand for. They also despise contempt."

"Vampires and werewolves partying together?" I shook my head. This event felt one step from carnage.

"Why not? I've met Gaian's type many times. They preach wanting to do the right thing and bettering the planet, but this is all about stroking his ego. He's playing up to a popular cause to show his dominance over supernaturals he can't possibly control."

"I'm not so sure," Zandra said. "Gaian's popular. People back him, and he quickly pulled in a crowd when he needed them."

"And there's a lot of tofu being served in that café. Gaian has a following," I said.

Remus bared his fangs. "It's a disgrace. I'm embarrassed for Sorcha."

"She's love struck," I said. "Gaian has her in his thrall."

"It's a thrall we must break. Local vampires have relied on her hospitality and kindness for a long time, and to have it taken so swiftly was a shock to the community. I've reached out to her more than once, but she's ignoring me."

"I keep hoping she'll come to her senses, but we almost got tossed out of the café when we saw her earlier," Zandra said. "She'll be with the protestors when they arrive."

Remus waved a hand in the air. "That saddens me. But the protesters don't bother me. Let them come, and we'll feast on their bones."

"There'll be no feasting on any bones, Remus Salamander." Cythera descended from the sky in a flutter of large white wings and feathers.

"Ah, of course. My favorite angel is here, ready to ensure law and order are met to the highest standards. I hope you'll save a space on your dance card for me, my dear. There'll be punk rock waltzing when the moon reaches its peak." Remus bowed at the waist and swept one hand behind him. "Angel Force is always welcome."

Her nostrils flared. "I've had complaints about you. Dozens of them."

"Let me guess. They're from out of towners who have no idea what this is all about?" I said. "And they said something vague about cruelty and hog roasts?"

Cythera barely spared me a glance. "There have been reports of imprisonments and people held against their will. I don't take information like that lightly."

Several more angels thudded to the ground in a showy display of white feathers, and stood behind Cythera, waiting for orders. I was pleased to see Finn among them. Although he winked at me, he stayed silent.

"Cythera! I'm wounded to my core. That's not how I run my hive. Everyone is here of their own free will. And everyone I turn, has passed the tests and signed the consent forms. I assure you, there is nothing untoward happening tonight," Remus said.

"I'll still need to look around and make sure these complaints are unjustified." Cythera's gaze swept across the growing crowd.

"My home is your home. I always have a bed made ready for you in case you ever need to spend the night."

A flush spread up Cythera's cheeks. "Stop being ridiculous and take this seriously. I could close this festival if I discover any infractions. I have the authority to do so."

"Yet, you won't. You're a benevolent angel, and you only want to see the right thing is done. Please, look around. And help yourselves to free food and drink. All my guests must feast until they're too full to move. That's what I intend to do."

"Uh-oh. Here comes trouble," I muttered.

The first gaggle of protestors appeared on the road on foot, drinks in hand, as they laughed and swayed.

"I don't see Gaian among them," Zandra said to me. "Or any of his gang members."

"This must be his advanced guard. I expect he'll arrive once more of his minions are in place, so he can have them bow before him."

"I met Gaian earlier today," Remus murmured, his attention on the group. "The man is impossible to reason with. And unpleasantly smug."

"You're talking about Sorcha's new companion?" Cythera said.

"Gaian Scythe is behind your problems and the false complaints about the Blood Moon Festival," I said. "He arranged for the protestors to be here. He's the troublemaker, not Remus."

"You're most kind to support me, you adorable floofy princess." Remus inclined his head in my direction.

"I wasn't aware of Gaian causing any problems." Cythera watched the crowd grow nearer.

"Because he's getting everyone else to do his dirty work," I said. "The more we learn about him, the less we trust him."

"Could I interest you fine people in some free brownies?" Edith arrived beside us, carrying a stacked tray of brownies, studded with dark chocolate chunks and drizzled in caramel sauce.

"I'm on duty." Cythera's gaze skittered over the brownies, and I didn't miss the way she licked her lips.

"I promise you won't find a better brownie within a ten-mile radius. Taste-test approved. My son, Drayton, tries my recipes. He's got a fine palate and always suggests tweaks so I can create perfection. He's a good boy."

I'd have protested the claim about how good the brownies were, but with the Gingerbread Bakery still closed for renovations following a devastating fire, I kept quiet.

"Stay away from her, you jerk! She came with me."

The raised male voice drew my attention, and I turned to see the pretty blonde in the tiny denim shorts who'd been outside Sorcha's café, pushing two guys apart as they blustered and swung at each other.

"Oh dear, they're still fighting." Edith lowered her tray of brownies. "I thought I'd gotten them to see sense."

"What are they fighting about?" Zandra said.

"That pretty young thing, of course," Edith said. "And she's not helping the situation. She keeps flirting with everybody. She even batted her lashes at me when I told her about my son. She asked if he was single!"

"Surely, she's allowed to flirt and flutter," I said. "She can bat her lashes and wiggle her behind as much as she likes and not face any consequences."

"Oh! Of course. I didn't mean that. Forgive a foolish old woman. I come from a different time, and my parents were so strict about how I behaved. I've tried to be lenient with my son, but it's not easy." Edith nudged a brownie into place with a fork. "That stunning young woman can behave as she likes. It's the gentlemen who get fired up and claim they can't control themselves."

"We'll see about that. I won't tolerate any harassment." Cythera strode away to quiet the dispute, gesturing for the rest of the angels to follow her.

We watched as they ended the fight and shooed the protestors along, ensuring the pretty blonde wasn't being bothered.

"The angels are letting them stay?" Zandra crouched beside me. "Shouldn't they send the protestors packing?"

"Freedom of speech and movement," I said. "And they haven't broken any laws that we know of."

"It's an opportunity for chaos and slaughter."

Remus gently cleared his throat. "Are you suggesting my vampires will misbehave?"

I looked up at him. "They have been known to break a few rules. And I include you in that statement."

He pressed one hand against his forehead. "You cut me with your cruelty."

Archie licked Remus's other hand. "Juno didn't mean it. Your vampires are always kind to me."

"You deserve that kindness." Remus petted Archie on the head.

We waited in silence as the group of protestors wandered past. They were half the number that had been at the café. Where were the rest? Making a stealth raid on the lobster tanks?

"Brownies, anyone? Freshly made. Make you smile." Edith bustled to the group, one brownie already speared on a fork.

The blonde in the tiny shorts stared at the tray and pushed it away. "Gross. I don't do carbs. Come on, hon, let's see what's happening." She grabbed one of the guys who'd been fighting over her and they sauntered away. "The first color dash is happening in a few minutes, and I won't miss it."

Edith's cheeks flushed. "There's nothing gross about my food."

Everyone else seemed to agree with her, and the tray was soon cleared as the group passed by. Even Finn snagged a brownie while Cythera had her back turned.

"Sorry about my sister." The stout young woman with the glasses I'd seen at the café smiled at Edith as she took the last brownie. "She's just excited. But I raised her better than that. And she eats carbs, she just pretends she doesn't because they make her bloat."

Edith set her brownie fork on the tray. "Oh, I don't mind. I know how high spirited you young people can be. I have one of my own. He sometimes needs a stern talking to when he gets stroppy."

The woman smiled. "I know how you feel. Your brownies look great."

"They are! Thank you. I have more on my stand. It's next to the face painting if you want to try more samples."

"Let's go, Dahlia! We don't want to miss out. Briar wants us to do the color dash. Hurry!"

She waved at an attractive woman with shorter hair who waited for her a short distance away. "My sisters! Briar and Primrose are so bossy, you'd think they were in charge of this family, but I'll be the one running around and making sure they behave. Enjoy the festival." Dahlia dashed off.

Edith stood with us a moment longer, smiling as music drifted out of hidden speakers and the buzz from the crowd grew. She nodded at us, then hurried to her stand, no doubt to stock up on more brownies.

Finn wandered over, wiping crumbs off his mouth and grinning. "Looks like it'll be a fun night once we get everyone calmed down."

Remus's gaze went to the sky, and he snarled. "It won't be unless that problem is dealt with."

My stomach dropped as the sky filled with protestors on motorbikes and broomsticks, and I rolled my eyes. "What's the point of flying in on something that has wheels?"

"They're showing off," Zandra said. "Making an entrance."

"It's an attempt at intimidation." Remus turned away. "If you'll excuse me. I must ensure everything is in place. Nothing will spoil the opening night of the festival. I'll be back soon."

The bikers and their broomstick riding companions swirled around our heads, engines roaring and broomsticks shaking. It was an impressively showy arrival, and must have taken potent magic to make them look coordinated. Perhaps I'd underestimated Gaian's powers.

The flying protestors finally landed, and Sorcha slid off Gaian's bike and grabbed placards to pass around.

Several blurs whipped past, and if it weren't for my finely attuned cat senses, the appearance of a dozen finely dressed vampires would have startled me. Remus was among them. The vampires formed a line while the protestors waved their placards.

Finn's smile slipped. "This could get ugly fast. I should see where Cythera is and what she wants us to do. She won't want this to escalate."

Remus stepped forward and adjusted his top hat. "Welcome to the Blood Moon Festival. I have fresh lobsters and hog roasts for you to enjoy. The meat is so tender, it falls off the bone. I expect you'll all want a taste."

"Murderer!" someone at the back of the group yelled.

"I've been called worse." Remus's smile appeared frozen, but it was there. "We plan to enjoy every second of the festival. Nothing, and let me be clear, nothing will get in our way of celebrating this most blessed event."

Cythera fluttered into view, her wings out. She took a second to view the scene before stepping in between the two groups. "Let's keep things civil."

"Always. You can depend on me to be the picture of civility." Remus bowed, but his attention didn't drift from Gaian, who still sat astride his bike, looking like he owned the place.

The two groups remained apart as more angels arrived, the glaring contests in full swing. Neither party budged.

"The animals demand compensation." Gaian stood at his full height beside his motorbike.

"I assure you, I get my creatures from the best suppliers. They have wonderful lives—"

"Until you rip them apart."

Remus drew in a slow breath. "My food is never ripped. And hog isn't my flavor of choice."

"You drain the living." A weedy female voice drifted from the group.

"I eat what I'm designed to eat. Food is not optional."

"Make a sizeable donation to an animal cause, and we'll leave you to your gross feasting," Gaian said.

Remus arched a neat eyebrow. "One you own, I assume?"

Gaian's mouth lifted at one corner. "Animals aren't owned by anyone. They should be free to roam as they please."

Remus tutted softly. "Think of the mess they'd make if we allowed them to do such a thing."

Gaian stepped forward, his hands lightly clenched. "This isn't a joke."

"Do you see me smiling?"

Archie whined and shoved his hot muzzle against my ear. "Should I bite Gaian? He's not being nice to Remus."

"Let's stay out of this for now and see what the angels do." I glanced toward the tempting scents drifting from a nearby hog roast, but forced myself to resist.

"This is my land," Remus said.

Gaian smirked. "Of course. The elite master, lording it over everyone else. I suppose you've got the angels in your pocket, too, and they'll arrest us for stepping on dirt that's been around a lot longer than you."

"What a delightful thought. Sadly, our branch of Angel Force has an incorruptible leader. Don't think I haven't attempted to offer the occasional bribe, but Cythera is not for turning."

"That's enough, Remus." Cythera was blushing again. "Will you all behave this evening, or do I have to shut this event?"

Gaian shrugged. "It can stay open. Remus knows my terms. Make reparations for the destruction of life, or we stay and make things difficult for him."

Remus stepped forward, his arms stiff by his sides. "Don't threaten me."

"I always promise, never threaten."

"Uh-oh," Finn muttered. "They're as stubborn as each other."

"Remus, please. We don't have to fight about this." Sorcha joined Gaian and wrapped an arm around his waist. "Do the right thing. No one wants to ruin this evening."

Remus's expression faltered and disappointment flickered in his eyes. "You're siding with him? But you love the Blood Moon Festival. Last year, you danced naked at the top of the turret. It was a beautiful sight to witness."

She glanced up at Gaian. "I'm... of course I'm on Gaian's side. I love him. And I love what he stands for."

Remus shook his head. "You've changed. You always looked after the vulnerable. Helped a vampire in their hour of need, or took in a stray familiar. But now... you abandon your cause for this guy? You abandon your heritage? Is he really worth it?"

"I am." Gaian raised his chin, a possessive look on his face as he held Sorcha close.

Sorcha bit her bottom lip, nodding but saying nothing.

No one spoke for several tense minutes, and the stalemate looked like it wasn't moving soon.

"This could take a while. I'm getting snacks," I whispered to Archie. "Bring you back anything?"

"I'm too nervous to eat. Wait! Maybe pork rinds. They do jumbo packs. I've already had three."

I dashed to the food stand selling porky treats, grabbed two bags of chunky pork rinds, and hurried back to join Archie.

"Did I miss anything?" I dropped a bag on the ground for him.

"Just Gaian talking about animal rights some more. He's even making me feel guilty for enjoying steak so much."

"Archie, you're a hellhound. You can't live on carrots. Neither can I. Eat your pork rinds."

He tore open the bag and got munching.

I sampled a meaty, greasy pork rind. "Gaian will have to back down. Even though there are fewer vampires here, he's outmatched in terms of power and speed."

"From the evil glint in his eyes, he's going nowhere," Archie mumbled, pork rind crumbs spraying from his mouth.

The accusations and debating continued for another half an hour as we ate and watched, watched and ate. Neither side moved, while Angel Force kept a watchful eye over things and cautioned anyone who got too vocal or red in the face.

Remus raised a hand. "That's enough! I tire of these distractions, and I demand our right to celebrate."

"We're not leaving," Gaian said. "And I have protestors planted around the festival. On my word, they'll spring into action."

"What will they do? Waft their patchouli cologne in people's faces and whack them with celery sticks if they spot them eating from the hog roasts?"

Gaian glowered at Remus. "They'll give you a festival you'll never forget."

Cythera flared her wings. "No more veiled threats."

"I agree." Remus tossed a glance at his hive. "Vampires, let's take the party inside. We'll get an amazing view of the moon from the turrets when it reaches its apex."

There was a cheer from the protesters, suggesting they smelled victory.

"Remus is backing down?" Zandra sounded as astonished as I felt.

Remus glanced at her, then lifted his shoulders slightly before returning his attention to the protesters. "My patience has worn out. Leave immediately, or I'll insist you're all arrested."

"What about the animals you hold captive and are at your mercy?" Gaian said.

"They'll be well treated until they meet their end. It's the best I can offer."

"That's not good enough."

Sorcha pressed a hand on Gaian's chest and looked up at him, a pleading expression on her face.

He sighed. "We'll give you space. But this isn't over."

"This bickering has given me an upset stomach." Archie danced on his paws, a noxious stench filling the air.

I backed away, wrinkling my booping snooter, and bumped into Zandra's feet. "That'll be the pork rinds, not the bickering."

"I'll be back in a few minutes." He dashed into the shadows of nearby trees.

Zandra crouched beside me. "This isn't the kind of fun we came for. Do you still want to party, or should we give the rest of the evening a miss? I wouldn't mind an early night and a movie. Even watching a back-to-back horror marathon would be less stressful than this."

"We've got to stay. The protesters could cause more trouble. And with the vampires and werewolves on the prowl, they need someone around to keep the peace."

"Isn't that what Angel Force is here for?"

I glanced up at my wonderful witch and leaned against her thigh. "We can still have fun tonight. I should get you a magical brownie. Then you'll loosen up."

"I'm loose! I mean, I'm not uptight. You know what I mean. I can party when I'm in the mood."

I chuckled. "We'll stay for an hour. If it's too intense, we'll leave. And you can pick the movie. Although I'm in the mood for a rom com with cats rather than a murder most foul."

"Deal."

Archie howled as he bolted out of the trees and pelted toward me.

My eyes widened. I could smell blood on his fur before I saw it. I dashed toward my anxious friend. "What happened? Are you hurt?"

"No! This blood isn't mine." He skidded to a halt. "I found a body!"

Chapter 4

Plucked rose

I raced back to the trees with Archie and Zandra. My senses pinged danger as long shadows stretched across the gloomy wood, masking any number of assailants.

"She's in here. I was relieving myself—I always get an upset stomach when Remus argues with someone—when I smelled something. I thought it was coming from me, but then I recognized the smell of blood. We get that same scent all the time at home, so I wasn't panicked, but thought I'd take a look. Make sure no one was hurt."

"Who is it?" Zandra pushed aside a tree branch as she continued to follow Archie.

"I don't know. She's not from around here. This way."

I leaped over a fallen tree and clambered a slight hill. Archie slowed and stepped to one side. He ducked his huge head and whimpered. In front of him lay the body of a blonde-haired woman.

I approached with caution, Zandra by my side. "She was with the protesters. I think someone called her Briar. I recognize those tiny denim shorts."

"And I recognize her from the café," Zandra said. "She was with that guy wearing all the eyeliner."

"And she had men fighting over her when she got here," I said.

"Look at her neck!" Archie whined. "She's been bitten."

"Vampire?" Zandra asked.

Archie closed his eyes. "I don't know. I hope not."

"Zandra, stay back so you don't contaminate the crime scene," I said.

She hesitated, her gaze on Briar. "What will you do?"

I coiled and leaped onto the victim's chest, so I wouldn't trample any evidence. The woman smelled of cedarwood, and her eyelids sparkled with pale shimmering shadow. Other than the two holes in her neck, there were no other injuries on her body. The paleness of her skin suggested most of her blood had been sucked from those holes.

"Did you see a vampire when you were in the woods?" Zandra said to Archie.

"No. There was no one else but me. When I got here, she was already like this." Archie lifted a paw, his body quivering. "And I didn't hear anyone run off."

"This draining happened recently," I murmured. "She's still warm."

Zandra looked around at the trees, but the shadows swallowed our surroundings, so anyone could be watching and we wouldn't know about it.

"I need Remus. He has to see this." Archie tipped back his head and howled, the noise sending a shudder through the trees and rumbling the dirt, magic pulsing around us.

Within two heartbeats, Remus flashed into view. "My hound. What is it? Your cry of distress speared my heart."

"There's been a vampire kill," Archie whispered. "A protester is dead."

Remus's head whipped around and he took in the scene, his mouth slightly open as if tasting the air. His lip curled, and he grimaced. "You're sure it was a vampire?"

I studied the holes in Briar's neck some more. "It looks like a bite from something with two fangs. And although I haven't done a thorough examination, I see no other injuries. And her waxy skin suggests she's missing the red stuff that kept her alive." Most of her skin was exposed, thanks to her lack of clothing, and although I could see odd smears of color across her flesh, they weren't bruises. They looked more like powdered paint.

Remus drew closer, his top hat clasped in his hands as he studied Briar. "This is unfortunate."

I cocked my head. "More than unfortunate. Did you know this woman?"

"We weren't acquainted. And I assure you, none of my vampires did this. They were looking forward to the turning and celebratory feasting. Why kill this woman when there is plenty of willing food waiting for us?"

"Then you have a rogue vampire on your hands," Zandra said.

"Not possible. I'd know if anyone had infiltrated my territory, and we've had no incursions. There's peace in this area." Remus's gaze remained on the victim.

"What's going on?" Cythera's voice echoed through the trees, sounding too close for comfort.

Remus tensed, then he sighed. "We can't keep this from Angel Force. They're bound to shut the festivities now."

Cythera yelped. "Blasted thorns! Where are you? Show yourselves, or I'll think you're up to no good."

"Cythera always thinks we're up to no good." I settled on Briar's chest and waited for the grumpy angel to appear.

"Over here," Zandra called. "We found something you need to see."

Cythera emerged from behind a tree with half a dozen angels, plucking twigs out of one wing. She stopped walking and stared at the body. She wasn't alone. Gaian, Sorcha, and several more protesters had followed the angels into the woods.

I grumbled to myself. The last thing we needed was Gaian's gaggle of protesters stirring things. And that's what they'd do when they saw one of them had fallen. Or rather, been drained and dumped by the enemy.

My gaze went to Gaian and my eyes narrowed. Would he sacrifice one of his own to ensure Remus couldn't host the Blood Moon Festival? He had more compassion for pigs than people. Maybe he'd decided one of his flock was a worthy sacrifice to ensure he got what he wanted.

"Finn, stay with the body," Cythera ordered. "And get that cat off her."

I rolled my eyes. Cythera knew my name, but she only used it when under extreme stress. "I touched nothing."

"You're standing on the corpse," she snapped. "Your paw prints will be all over her!"

"Sorry, Juno. I need you out of here." Finn held his hands out, ready to catch me if I jumped, but I nimbly leaped off, landing several feet from Briar's body. "It appears she's been bitten."

Finn stood back as he took in the scene. "I see that. Any more bite marks on her?"

"Two single holes on the side of her neck," I said. "And there's barely any blood. I'd say she's been drained."

Finn completed a slow circuit around Briar, his gaze sweeping the area. "There are no signs of a struggle. She must have bared her neck."

"Or been compelled to let someone feed from her."

Finn's mouth twisted from side to side and he glanced at the onlookers.

"That's Briar Vixen!" Gaian still had his arm around Sorcha.

"Did you say Briar's here? She'd better not be drunk again." The mousy woman I'd seen with Briar pushed past the watchers, holding another woman's hand.

"Don't look." Gaian reached for her shoulder, but she'd already moved past him.

The color drained from her face, and a strangled note slid from her lips. "Is she..."

"Don't get any closer." Cythera hurried over and blocked the view. "Do you know this woman?"

"It's our sister, Briar Vixen. I'm Dahlia. This is Primrose." Dahlia tried to dodge around Cythera, but she stopped her. "I've been looking for Briar since the color dash. She got paint in her eyes and needed to wash them out. What's wrong? Is she hurt?"

Primrose stood on her tiptoes, failing to look over Cythera's shoulder. "When Briar didn't come back, I figured she'd hooked up with someone. Is she dead?"

"Hush! She's not dead." Dahlia's skin faded to a grayish-green. "Is she?"

"I'm sorry," Cythera said.

Dahlia swayed a few times, then fainted, only saved from hitting the ground by Finn's speedy move as he caught her and lowered her slowly to the dirt.

Cythera called forward more angels. "Secure the scene and make sure no one else goes near the body. Then clear the people out of here. We need no further evidence contamination." Her gaze cut to me.

I looked away, not responding to her angry glare.

"Remus, I need to speak to your vampires," Cythera said.

"Why would that be, my most illustrious angel?"

"The holes in Briar's neck suggest one of them did this. I intend to find out who it was."

"It wasn't anyone in my hive." Remus stood firm, his legs slightly apart. "Besides, they wouldn't associate with someone of this caliber."

"What do you mean by that?" Red dots of anger popped onto Gaian's face. "Briar was a great girl. Life and soul of the party until one of you drained her."

Remus snorted a note of displeasure. "We have twenty-four willing, suitable, and intellectually advanced individuals begging to be turned under the blood moon. It's food on tap tonight. We don't feast on the desperate."

"You're saying Briar was dumb?"

"Actually, I said desperate. But if you want to add dumb to the mix, be my guest."

"Freakin' disrespectful vampire!" Gaian dodged past an angel who was attempting to turn him away and ran at Remus.

Finn stepped forward and held Gaian back. "You'll get yourself arrested if you keep going."

"A woman's dead and he's mocking her!"

A glitter of fury flooded Remus's eyes. He blinked, and it was gone. "I'm saying my hive had no need to associate with this poor creature. There's no motive for them to attend an unauthorized feast. They know better than that."

"Because you've trained them to fear you?" Gaian said. "That's how you run things around here?"

Remus hissed and his fangs flashed into view. "My vampires are well treated and cared for, no matter what they do."

"Meaning you'll cover for the one who did this to Briar." Gaian shook his head. "Typical vampires. Always keeping secrets."

"Someone's not a vampire fan," I muttered to Zandra, while petting Archie with one paw to ease his perpetual whine.

"Remus, step down. You're aggravating this situation." Cythera stalked over, abandoning her task of moving staring lingerers who wanted another look at the body.

"My sweet angel, we are on my land, at my festival, and I'm defending the honor of my hive. I will not step down, apologize, or retreat. In fact, I'll do the opposite." Remus closed his eyes and spread his arms. And although he made no sound, the trees rustled wildly as if twisting in a strong breeze, and I caught a whiff of dust and decay.

A moment later, the air was alive with the flutter of bat wings whipping through the black sky. They were accompanied by swirls of fog as twenty vampires materialized. They swarmed around Remus, their fisted hands and tight shoulders showing they knew they weren't here for an impromptu dance party by moonlight.

"Summoning your hive will only inflame the situation." Cythera's wings quivered.

"Too late for that." Zandra scooped me into her arms and settled me on her shoulder while resting her free hand on Archie's head. "Hey, buddy. It'll be okay. We'll figure this out."

"With minimal bloodshed," I said.

"No bloodshed!" Zandra side-eyed me.

I shrugged. We were dealing with vampires. Blood to them was like water.

"Cythera is looking at Remus as if she thinks he's guilty of killing that lady," Archie said. "I know he didn't do this. He's got his favorite meal picked out at the turning. I even met him. The guy smells like hamburgers, and he's huge and meaty. Remus said he reminded him of a walking ham hock and he couldn't wait to tuck in."

"A disturbingly delicious description," I said.

Zandra huffed a laugh. "Or we could just stop with disturbing."

"It's an excellent choice of meal," I said. "And is proof Remus is innocent. Besides, when did he have a chance to drain Briar? He's been bickering with Gaian."

"It wasn't him," Archie said. "He's a good vampire."

Archie's devotion to his vampire companion was admirable, but Remus had a dark side. I just hoped he hadn't let it loose on Briar as revenge against the protestors messing with his Blood Moon Festival.

Magic sparked among the remaining protesters, and the vampires growled and hissed. Any second, the thin thread of control would snap, quickly followed by several necks if the angels didn't move quickly.

Finn stepped between the two groups, his wings out and light red sparkles flickering across his feathers, revealing his demon side simmered just beneath the surface.

Archie bounded toward Finn, and for a second, I thought he'd leap on him, but he stood by Finn's side, his fur puffed out and his hellhound energy flickering off him in waves of purple flame. The two were an impressive sight and made an effective blockade between the groups.

"Archie, my perfect fluffy companion, as much as I adore your help, this isn't your fight," Remus said. "Come away before someone harms you and breaks my heart."

Archie whined, but held firm in his position beside Finn.

"No one is fighting anyone," Finn said. "I understand why tensions are high, but we'll get nowhere if you're feuding. And if a fight takes place here, all evidence of what happened to Briar will be destroyed, and her killer will never be found. Does anyone want that to happen?"

"The killer does," I muttered.

"Your attacker stands before you." Gaian jabbed a finger at Remus.

Remus snarled, his eyes flashing as his control slipped. "I didn't kill this woman."

"If not you, then you ordered one of your vampires to do it. That makes you as guilty as if you stuck in your own fangs."

"If you insult my hive once more, we'll have every right to tear you to shreds. You're on our land, in our territory, and you've disrespected us. Vampire law stands here—"

"No, it doesn't." Cythera stood beside Finn, casting a wary eye at Archie as he continued to growl. A purple flame flickered from his mouth, almost catching her wing alight. She blew out the spark and scowled at him. "You'll respect universal magical law. And Finn is correct. This is a crime scene. We must be able to do our jobs so we can find out what happened to Briar. If anyone prevents that, they'll become prime suspect in this investigation."

Gaian opened his mouth to protest, but Sorcha tugged his arm and shook her head. He remained silent. It was good to see she had a small amount of control over him, even if she couldn't control him getting rid of everything delicious in her café.

"Remus, I know you're angry, but we need to respect the dead," Finn said.

Archie nodded. "And this nice lady deserves justice."

"Your hellhound speaks the truth," Cythera said. "Listen to him, unless you want to spend the night in a cell."

Although anger simmered off Remus and his fangs remained on display, he slowly nodded. "I will send my vampires home, so long as the protesters retreat."

"We're going nowhere until we find out what happened to Briar," Gaian said.

"We can go to the café and wait there for news," Sorcha said. "Angel Force needs to focus. If we wait around, we'll only get in the way and slow things down."

Gaian looked at his gang and the remaining protestors. His attention settled on Dahlia, who had roused, but remained on the ground. "Dahlia, Briar was your sister. What do you want us to do? Stay or go? We'll fight if we have to. Just say the word, and we'll defend your sister's honor."

I resisted the urge to roll my eyes. This jerk was spoiling for a fight.

Finn folded his wings back into place, all traces of his demon power gone. He helped Dahlia to her feet, keeping a hold of her. "Take it easy. You've had a shock."

Dahlia gulped in several breaths, still looking deathly pale. "Briar's really gone? I didn't imagine it?"

Primrose sidled over to her. "I knew something like this would happen to Briar. She always had to show off and be the center of attention."

Dahlia glared at her. "Not now."

"But—"

"No! Briar is dead!" Dahlia swayed again.

"I'm sorry for your loss," Finn said. "We need to investigate the scene, though, and staying will only make it hard for us to do that."

Primrose shrugged. She glanced at Briar, her eyes hazing for a second. "We should let them get on. Briar would want this figured out."

Dahlia nodded. "Why do this? She only ever wanted to have fun. She meant no harm when she got over excited. Briar was just high spirited."

"It sounds as if Briar's sisters were worried about her behavior," I muttered into Zandra's ear. "She could have been putting herself in risky situations."

Zandra nodded, her attention on the vampires and protestors.

"Let's go to the café," Gaian said, after he'd glared at Remus some more. "Primrose, Dahlia, you stay with us. We'll look after you."

"Yes! Stay at the café," Sorcha said. "I have a room at the back you can use."

"Thanks. We've got a tent we were planning on staying in, but..." Dahlia licked her lips. "I'm not sure I'd feel safe."

"Of course not. Stay with me." Sorcha rushed over and took hold of their hands. "You don't want to camp here after what happened to your sister. You need comfort. A hot shower, tea, and a warm bed."

"Finn, take these ladies to the café and ensure they're settled in," Cythera said. She gestured for him to step away with her out of earshot of the protestors, but closer to us. "Are you in control of yourself? I noticed your energy was unstable."

My ears flicked as I listened in. Finn had issues with his demon side, but he'd successfully managed that darker part of him for months.

He gave a sharp nod. "Of course. Everyone was on edge, and it got me agitated."

"You did well. Good job." Cythera touched his shoulder. "While you're with Primrose and Dahlia, check what they've been doing in the last couple of hours. We must figure out Briar's last movements and if she had problems with anyone. Her sisters included."

"You got it, boss."

Cythera's gaze landed on Archie. "What's that on your fur? Blood?"

He jerked his head back. "No! I mean, yes! I... I found her. I checked if she was hurt."

Cythera stalked toward him. "That's Briar's blood?"

Gaian had been moving the protestors away, but they all stopped to watch the confrontation.

Remus whirled on his heel and stormed over to Archie. "Do not come for my hound. Of course, he'd do nothing like this. He's a gentle creature."

"He would if you ordered him to kill. Archie is in your thrall just as your hive vampires are." Cythera fluttered her wings.

I jumped off Zandra's shoulder and stepped in front of Archie as he whimpered and cowered. For all his might and looming appearance, he was a sweetheart, and one sharp word from Cythera had his giant paws quivering and his words failing. "I'm happy to alibi for Archie. We've been together since I arrived at the festival. The only time I left his side was to get pork rinds. Maybe three minutes at the most. That's not enough time to have done this."

Cythera puckered her lips. "You weren't together when Archie found the body?"

"I don't watch my friends when they have emergency toilet situations. It's not polite. Archie got blood on his fur because he found Briar and wanted to check she was okay and if he could help her. Archie is a good boy."

He thumped his tail in the dirt. "The best boy. Not a killer. I wanted to help this lady. I only sniffed her. That's when my fur must have touched the holes on her neck."

Cythera inhaled through her nose and let the breath out slowly. "I shall need a statement from you, Archie."

"And he's more than happy to give you one, so long as you don't accuse him of something he didn't do." Remus glowered at Cythera. "My hound's taste is impeccable when it comes to his food. This would never be his meal of choice. Remus loves his steak and hog roasts."

Cythera's gaze latched onto Remus. "If it wasn't your hound, and since there are clearly vampire bites on the victim, where were you?"

Chapter 5

Vampire accused

I grimaced. Cythera was playing with vampire fire by continuing this line of questioning.

Remus struggled to contain himself before letting out a tight breath. "As you are well aware, I was arguing with that idiot." He gestured at Gaian, who was still watching.

"Before that." Cythera raised a hand. "Wait. Let's do this properly. Angels, move the protesters back to the main site and speak to them. See if anyone saw anything suspicious. And we need contact details for the victim's family."

"That's us," Dahlia said. "We're Briar's only family."

"Your parents?"

She shook her head. "It's just us."

"Very well. I'll need to speak to you both at our office. Wait with an angel."

"I thought we were going to the café?" Primrose said.

"You can soon. I won't keep you long," Cythera said.

We waited in a tense silence as the angels slowly directed the protesters away. I took note that Gaian was the last to leave, a smug look on his face as he snuggled a worried Sorcha against him.

"He thinks he's won," I said to Zandra. "Look at him. The Blood Moon Festival is over because of Briar's murder."

"And Remus and his hive are under suspicion," Zandra said. "Coincidence?"

"I wondered the same thing. We need to do more digging into Gaian."

"And I'm happy to join you in that digging," Remus murmured, a hand resting on Archie's head as he continued to tremble. "A murder has been committed on my land, and I can't let that go unpunished. And I promise you this: it wasn't me or any of my vampires who drained this woman."

"Then explain this to me." Cythera had been crouched next to Briar, conducting a visual examination of the scene.

"What have you got?" I trotted over to get a closer look at what Cythera had found. A pink silk handkerchief was in one of Briar's clenched hands.

"Remus, is this yours?" Cythera asked.

Remus stood behind me with Archie beside him. "Lots of people carry handkerchiefs."

"You always have one in your top pocket. But not tonight. Why is that?" Cythera stood, her gaze on Remus's empty top pocket.

His hand went to his pocket, and he patted it several times. "Perhaps because of all the excitement, I forgot to finish my dress. There's been a lot to think about."

"Or during your fight with the victim, she grabbed it."

"That's making a whopper of an assumption," I said. "That handkerchief could belong to anybody."

Cythera didn't look at me. "Remus has a unique style of dress. I know no one else in the area who walks around with silken handkerchiefs and cravats."

"Even if that handkerchief turns out to be his, he could have dropped it, or given it to Briar. There are many reasons why she's holding it, yet you jump to the conclusion it was in her hand because they fought." I glanced at Remus. It was rare to see him looking uncomfortable, but I could see his concern. He wouldn't have done this. He didn't know Briar. And why be so careless as to leave her body where anyone would find it, with marks of a vampire bite on display? It was careless, and that was something Remus was definitely not.

"You always color coordinate. And this handkerchief matches your outfit." Cythera stood and brushed down her knees. "So, I'll ask you again, did you have anything to do with this woman being found here tonight?"

"No! Her death has nothing to do with me."

His vampire hive, who'd been silently watching, surged to life and surrounded Remus.

"We'll vouch for him," one of them said.

"We were there when he was arguing with the protesters," another said. "He didn't do this."

"Remus didn't know her."

"She's not his type."

"Your words mean nothing to me," Cythera said. "You'll all say anything to ensure your master stays safe. He's compelled you to do that."

That cutting remark earned her several hisses and growls.

Remus lifted a hand. "Calm yourselves. Your support is appreciated, but not needed. Cythera saw me with her own eyes. And although I am a magnificent supernatural being, I can't be in two places at once. I was either arguing with the protesters or murdering this young woman."

"Before that," Cythera said. "Where were you before Gaian showed up at the festival?"

"It's not relevant," I said.

Cythera slid a glare my way. "Why is that?"

"Briar's been dead for less than an hour."

"You're a forensic expert now?" She tutted. "Leave the investigative work to the professionals. We'll soon have Briar examined and can determine when she died."

"When I sat on her, she was still warm," I said. "Remus couldn't have done this. He didn't have the time."

"Remus, answer my question," Cythera said. "Before the protesters arrived, and you confronted them, what were you doing?"

"Perhaps we should take this to an interview room, just as you suggested." Finn's tone was diplomatic, and he kept his wings folded tightly against his body. "If Remus is considered a suspect, we should get everything on record as soon as possible."

Cythera's cheeks flushed. "Of course. That's what I meant to do. He distracted me. Take him now. I'll finish here and join you for the interview. Don't start without me."

I glanced at Zandra. It wasn't uncommon to see Cythera flustered in situations like this, but she seemed more flustered than usual. Was having to deal with the protesters and a hive of vampires too much for her?

"I insist Juno and Zandra help in this matter," Remus said. "I trust them to be fair, thorough, and ensure justice is done."

"There's no need for amateurs to be involved," Cythera said.

Remus tugged on his jacket cuffs. "I'm permitted representation. That's who I choose to represent me."

"You want a young witch with no legal experience and a cat who has an ego bigger than the size of your home to ensure you get off a murder charge?"

Zandra smirked and crossed her arms over her chest while I examined one of my magnificent paws.

"You underestimate them to your detriment," Remus said. "Since they moved to Crimson Cove, this has become a much safer place."

"A more murderous place, you mean. The cases never stop landing on my desk."

"Perhaps the crimes were being committed, but you ignored them," I said. "We'd never do that."

Cythera flared her wings. "Stay out of my way. Finn, take Remus and Archie to an interview room."

"What will happen to our sister?" Dahlia said quietly.

Cythera's expression softened. "We'll gather what evidence we can and then take Briar to the station. I'll have an expert examine her to see what more we can learn. You'll be kept informed. But for now, please follow Finn to the station. We won't keep you long. Then you can go to the café."

Primrose and Dahlia stared at their sister's body for a second, then turned and walked away, hand in hand.

I nodded at Remus, before he was escorted away by another angel, Archie by his side.

Cythera turned and her gaze ran over me and Zandra. "You're still here? Don't you want to go with your new client?"

"We figured we could help you look for evidence," I said.

"No help is needed. You're assisting Remus, not me." She marched away and got the rest of her angels scouring the area for clues.

"With all the people who've tramped through here, you'll be fortunate to find anything useful," I said. "A keen booping snooter could be just what you need to crack this case."

Cythera ignored me as she looked behind a rotting tree stump.

"What's up with her?" Zandra whispered. "She's usually grumpy, but this is next level grump."

"I'm unsure. She seems flustered, too. Maybe she needs a vacation."

"What I need is to not be hassled by amateurs who think they know how to do my job." Cythera had her back to us as she stared at something on the ground.

"If we're your only problem, then your life is rosy," I said. "Don't shut us out. You know we can do good."

She walked over to Briar, and after a few seconds of silence, she nodded. "What do you see here?"

I hurried over and looked at Briar. "First glance? It looks like a classic vampire bite and drain."

"So, we agree. Remus, or a member of his hive, did this."

"We don't agree on that," I said. "And it couldn't have been Remus. We all saw him."

"That doesn't mean he didn't order the kill," Cythera said. "That makes him almost as guilty as whoever sank their fangs into this young lady."

"Perhaps when Briar's body has been examined, I could take another look?" I said. "Figure this out for you. My expert opinion is always available whenever you need it."

She rasped out her disgust. "Get out of here. Go represent your vampire. I'll be along shortly. Don't begin the interview without me."

"We should do as she says," Zandra whispered to me. "We're only making her grumpier by sticking around. And I want to see how Remus is getting on."

I trusted the angels to do a reasonable job of clue gathering, and having already had a look at the body, I didn't think I'd learn anything new if we stayed.

After returning to Crimson Cove and going straight to Angel Force, Zandra grabbed a coffee and snacks from the kitchen, and we found Finn settling Remus into an interview room. Finn walked out and pulled the door closed behind him.

"How's he doing?" I said.

"He keeps saying he's innocent," Finn said.

"I believe him. I know Cythera thinks Remus could have done this earlier in the evening, but I don't see how or why. And when he holds a party, he's always at the center of everything. He wouldn't have had the time or inclination to sneak off and drink from a stranger."

"And as I keep saying, I have twenty-four willing meals waiting for me in the mansion," Remus called from the interview room.

"Stop using your vampire hearing," Finn said. "I'll get you a drink, and then we'll wait for Cythera to get back before starting the interview."

"I'm here." She strode through the door and into the open-plan office. "Let's get going. It's already late, and the overtime bill will cripple me."

Remus nudged open the door. "I'll have my O Positive warm, if you don't mind."

Cythera marched into the interview room with Finn behind her, and after shooting us a quick look and gesturing to the room next to us, she closed the door in our faces.

"I guess that means we're not Remus's official legal representation," I said.

"We're the tolerated representation. You could always protest about her rude behavior." Zandra stifled a yawn behind one hand.

"It would only slow things. Let's grab a seat, hear what Remus has to say, and then call it a night."

Zandra's lack of protest showed she was tiring, and a quick check of the wall clock revealed we'd just slid past midnight. My witch needed her sleep, or she'd be grumpy, too.

Once we were settled in our seats, watching the interview through the one-way mirrored glass, and Cythera had run through the formalities, she got straight to the questioning.

Remus repeated his alibi and stated he didn't kill Briar.

"Did you have any issue with her?" Cythera said.

"I didn't know her. The protesters were an unwelcome addition to the Blood Moon festivities."

"When did you meet Briar?"

"I never said I did." Remus clicked his tongue. "I first noticed the protestors' pungent presence the morning before the festival, when several showed up with grubby tents. Of course, being an amenable host, I asked if they needed anything. That's when I learned what Gaian and his gang had in store for my event. Briar wasn't there, though."

"Their arrival must have made you angry," Cythera said.

"More like frustrated. I've been looking forward to this festival for months. It's the pinnacle of vampiric celebration, when the Blood Moon sails high in the sky, containing hints of the glorious color of our sustenance. It's important we worship that and show the proper respect to our power."

"The protesters were hoping to spoil things for you?"

"They could have attempted to ruin the fun, but if things had gotten out of hand, I had the law on my side." Remus's smile was innocent, but there was a glint of mischief in his eyes. "I could have had them removed for trespassing if I considered them a threat."

"So, instead of compromising with them, you antagonized them," Cythera said.

"Did I?"

"I'm aware of the twelve new turning orders you submitted to the Vampire Council. I also noticed the trucks rumbling through Crimson Cove with your extra hog roasts. And I heard rumors there were lobster tanks and lambs delivered. Those weren't acts of antagonism?"

"Remus is pushing his luck with Cythera," Zandra said. "He's trying not to laugh at being caught out."

"There is a grim humor here," I said. "And Remus always enjoys getting a rise out of people."

"He shouldn't. Not when he's a murder suspect."

"I'll confess to those minor amusements," Remus said. "I don't like it when somebody spoils my fun, but I broke no laws. Gaian and his friends have their way of living, and we have ours. Our vampire lifestyle isn't perverted, it's how we're supposed to live. I did nothing wrong."

"Did Briar get in the way of you living your best life?" Cythera asked.

"I didn't even notice her among the protestors. The first time I was aware of her being at the event was when her body was found in my woods."

Cythera leaned forward. "Where were you before you confronted the protesters?"

Remus shifted in his seat and glanced at Archie, who sat close to his side, his ears up, taking in everything. "In my bedroom. I was planning a surprise for Archie."

"You were?" Archie said.

"I wanted to treat you. I got you a special gift and needed to set it up. But it was hard to get a moment alone in the lead up to the festival. I fibbed to some of my vampires and said I wanted to change my outfit before it got busy, then slipped away."

"Were you with anyone?" Cythera said.

"No. I did this on my own."

"Then you have no alibi."

"Wrong. You're my alibi. You saw me arguing with the protestors when Briar was being drained."

Cythera was quiet for a few seconds. She glanced at Finn. "Once we've examined Briar's body, we'll be able to determine the time of her death. It's still possible you did this."

"Even with an examination of her body, they won't be able to pin the time of death to an exact minute," I murmured. "And as I keep telling Cythera, Briar was warm when I sat on her chest. And a body with no blood in it cools quickly."

"That's gruesome knowledge to have." Zandra shuddered.

"Handy knowledge. It means Archie only just missed the killing happening. That'll help get Remus off the suspect list."

"If you didn't know Briar, why was your handkerchief clutched in her hand?" Cythera said.

I leaned forward when she asked that question. Cythera had made a valid point about Remus being the only resident who carried silken hankies in his top pocket.

He hesitated before patting his empty pocket again. "Perhaps I dropped it and Briar picked it up. It's a lovely color."

"Or it was grabbed during the struggle."

"What struggle? I'll return you to my twenty-four willing, warm, and delicious meals waiting to be turned. I had no need to grab a snack." Remus let out a soft sigh. "They must be wondering what's going on. The turning was due to happen at midnight. They'll be so disappointed."

"Which means you must be hungry," Cythera said.

"Just the opposite. Prior to a turning event, I always ensure I'm satisfied. If I lose control while turning an individual into a vampire, I risk draining them of essential nutrients. You can't turn a husk into an immortal creature, so I need to stop feeding at the right time." He spread his hands. "Even if I was hungry, I'd never pick a skinny vegan to feast on. There'd be no taste to that meal."

"He has a point," I said. "I doubt a plant muncher would make a tasty snack."

Cythera sat back in her seat. She seemed at a loss for what to say. Hopefully, she realized her error and was about to release Remus.

Archie whimpered. "Can we go home now?"

"Soon, my marvelous furry forever friend." Remus scratched Archie's head. "Cythera, we've been through a lot together during my habitation in Oak Park Ridge. I know you don't always approve of my way of life, but I've never maliciously caused you trouble. And I haven't done it now. I didn't kill Briar."

She massaged the bridge of her nose. "You're still a suspect. And a flight risk."

Finn looked at her in surprise. "Remus wouldn't run."

"Of course I wouldn't." Remus's fingers flexed on Archie's head. "You can't lock me up for this. You don't have enough evidence."

"What if I let you go and you disappear?" Cythera asked.

He eased back in his seat. "Ah, you're worried I'll turn into a bat or fog and drift away on the air currents and you'll never see me again."

"You could flee to save yourself. The evidence we have so far means it's not looking good for you."

"I won't deny there are elements to this mystery that suggest a vampire could be involved." Remus rested his hands on the table. "But I have too much to lose by leaving. My hive is here. My adorable pup, and my friends." He glanced at the mirror and winked. "Let me go. I'll return home and stay out of trouble."

Cythera tapped her fingers on the table. "You can leave, but I'll assign an Angel Force guard at your mansion. Those are my conditions."

Remus pressed his lips together, then nodded. "With my excellent representation, they'll have this figured out within hours. Then I'll expect an apology. Do you compensate those you've wrongly accused of murder?"

Cythera stood and gave him a hard stare. "I'll be in touch."

"I look forward to it, dear angel."

I hopped onto Zandra's lap. "It's time to get sleuthing."

Chapter 6

Family connection

Once Cythera wrapped up the interview with Remus, he'd been allowed to return home with Archie. I was about to suggest we go home too, but Zandra headed to the kitchen and poured herself another coffee.

"We'll wrap this up soon." Finn joined us and accepted a steaming mug from her. "Briar's body won't be examined until the morning, but we want to interview her sisters while any useful information is fresh in their minds. You don't have to stay, though. I can fill you in tomorrow."

"We should go. You're dead on your feet," I said to Zandra.

"No, I want to stay. Remus has been good to us, so I'd like to find out what happened and make sure he doesn't get in anymore trouble."

"He will if he keeps running his mouth. Cythera isn't amused," Finn said.

"She rarely is," I murmured.

Zandra pursed her lips. "I'm not happy how Cythera seems so convinced he's involved." She glanced at Finn. "What's up with her, anyway?"

"Not sure. She's been snapping for days. I thought it was work stress, but there's something else on her mind. No point asking what it is, though. She shuts down questions."

I looked at her closed office door. That grumpy angel needed a friend.

"She's dealing with the paperwork, so you're welcome to sit in on the interviews with the sisters. We're starting with Dahlia."

"The nervous one who fainted?" I asked.

"That's the one."

"We'll bring the smelling salts."

It took a few minutes, and plenty of gentle reassurance, before Dahlia was willing to be separated from Primrose. They'd been sitting quietly in a couple of chairs, clutching each other's hands and murmuring while Remus had been interviewed.

Once Dahlia was settled in a seat with a mug of herbal tea in front of her, and Finn had made the introductions, he began the interview.

"Please confirm your name for me," Finn said.

"Dahlia Vixen."

"And your relation to Briar Vixen?"

"Her older sister. Older by five years. She was the middle sister. Primrose is the baby of the bunch."

"And why were you in Crimson Cove?" Finn said.

Dahlia picked up her tea and splashed it across the back of her hand, almost dropping the mug. "Sorry! I can't stop shaking. I keep seeing Briar on the ground, not moving." She gulped and ducked her head.

Finn wiped up the spilled liquid. "No need to apologize. You've had a huge shock."

"Could you tell us about your relationship with your sister?" I asked.

Dahlia hesitated. "It was complicated. I love my sisters and I wouldn't be without them, but we haven't had an easy time. I raised Briar and Primrose."

"Where are your parents?" Zandra said.

"Gone. I'd just turned eighteen when they died in an accident. They were botanical wizards. Anything green they touched would blossom. One day, though, they touched something they shouldn't. A rare portal strangler tree ate them and there was nothing left but a few gold teeth."

I opened my mouth, but could think of nothing helpful to say.

"Sorry to hear that," Finn said after a few seconds of awkward silence.

Dahlia accepted the words with a small sigh. "I was still a dumb kid, but suddenly I was expected to raise my sisters. I wasn't ready, and I didn't want to do it. But I had no choice. Well, I had the choice of putting them into care, but I couldn't do that."

"That must have been a terrible shock for your whole family," Finn said. "Was there no one else who could help you?"

"It was just the five of us for a long time. No grandparents or aunts and uncles alive. Our parents were wealthy, though. They left us a big house and plenty of money, so that wasn't a concern. But I had no parenting skills, yet I got landed with two teenagers I was supposed to mold into functioning adults." Dahlia pushed her glasses up her nose. "And Primrose was just coming into her botanical powers. Not that any of us have much power to write home about, but I had to figure out how to steer her right and make sure she didn't mess with something that would poison her or eat her, too. It was overwhelming."

"It looks like you managed just fine," Finn said. "You seem close."

"Sometimes, but I always felt the boundaries got blurred. I didn't want to be a parent. I wanted to be a big sister, but if I fooled around and didn't take things seriously, bills weren't paid, the house became a mess, and my sisters went wild."

"So, you stepped up?" I asked. "That was decent of you."

"You had to give up the fun and take on a role you weren't ready for," Zandra said. "Sounds tough."

"There were moments when I wondered what I was doing." A wobbly smile lifted Dahlia's face. "But it was important we stayed together. Briar and Primrose are the only family I have. Well, now I only have Primrose." Tears spilled from her eyes as she lowered her head.

"What was Briar's relationship like with Primrose?" Finn said.

Dahlia puffed out a breath. "Spiky. They loved to argue. Honestly, they'd argue over anything from hairbrushes to world politics."

"They didn't like each other?" Zandra said.

"It was a sister thing. You must know what it's like if you've got sisters."

Zandra half-smiled. "Sure. I know what you mean. You love them, but you still want to strangle them when they're bossing you around."

"Exactly! We love each other and we'd do anything for each other, but we also sometimes want to slap each other's faces. We never mean it. There was always that core of love that kept us together."

Dahlia sounded genuine in her equal care and frustration for her siblings.

"Do you know what Briar was doing in the woods at the festival?" Finn said. "Was it normal for her to go off alone?"

"No. She was a social butterfly, and loved to be the center of attention, so I doubt she'd have gone into the woods on her own. If she was ever alone for more than an hour, she got depressed." Dahlia smiled sadly. "I'm the opposite. I like quiet time. It was another thing we clashed over. Primrose was our intermediary. When I needed peace, and Briar was being too intense, I'd send her to find Primrose. It usually worked."

"You think Briar went into the woods with someone?" Finn said.

"I'm certain. And I've been thinking about when I saw her last."

"When was that?"

Dahlia wriggled her nose from side to side, her gaze on the ceiling. "We got food, and Briar was complaining about all the guys paying her attention. Honestly, it was typical Briar behavior. She'd flirt and giggle, and then wonder why they wanted her number. And the length of her shorts left little to the imagination. I kept telling her to change, but she ignored me."

"She was single?" I asked.

"No, she brought her boyfriend with her. Well, they weren't exclusive, but he was her latest favorite guy."

"Could she have been with him?"

"It's possible. I'm not sure where Trent was all evening, though. Same goes for Briar. She could never sit still."

That was a new name for the suspect list.

"Where were you when you heard what happened to Briar?" Finn said.

"I didn't know what had happened to her at first, but I followed the crowd when they headed into the woods. I heard someone say something weird was going on. That was when I saw her."

"And before that, what were you doing?"

Dahlia dabbed at tears on her cheeks. "Walking around on my own. I hadn't seen Briar for a while. She'd gone off to have fun in the second color dash. That's not my thing, so I didn't get involved. Too messy for me."

"What's a color dash?" Zandra said.

"It originated from a Hindu celebration of throwing powdered paints to celebrate spring and goodness. In the magic community, we throw small balls of powdered paint containing a fun spell. Nothing damaging. Sometimes, a tickle or laughter spell." Dahlia attempted a smile. "It's too boisterous for me. I'm a 'curl up with a book and a hot chocolate' kind of girl. But Primrose and Briar were excited to take part. Briar had already been through one color dash."

"That would explain the color on her skin," I said. "I noticed it when we found her in the woods."

"Briar was always drawn to fun. The louder, the better. I had no idea..." she took several seconds to compose herself. "I had no idea it was Briar who'd been hurt."

"We're sorry about what happened to her," Zandra said.

Dahlia nodded. "I'd like to see her. Say a proper goodbye. I didn't get a chance when we were in the woods. I was so shocked. And I had to keep an eye on Primrose. She doesn't handle stress well."

"You'll be able to see Briar soon. But we need to run tests to figure out exactly what happened to her," Finn said.

Dahlia blinked several times. "She was bitten by a vampire, wasn't she? That's what everyone said. And I saw the marks on her neck. What else could have done that to her?"

"We'll have answers for you soon enough." Finn put down his pen. "Have you got someone who can stay with you, other than Primrose? You two shouldn't be alone."

"No, we came here, just the three of us, not including Trent. That's how it's been for a long time."

"Sorcha will look after you," Zandra said. "And her café is great. She'll make sure you're comfortable and have everything you need."

Dahlia pressed her fingers against her forehead. "I was stupid to agree to come to this festival. Briar's been into vampires since she was a child. I should have put my foot down and said no. I should have known something bad would happen. She was my responsibility, and I let her down."

"No one could predict this," Finn said.

"It was only a matter of time, wasn't it? She was always taking risks and looking for the next adventure. Now, I've lost my sister." Dahlia broke into ragged sobs, and we could do nothing but sit in an uncomfortable silence and watch Finn's gentle words doing nothing to stop the flood of tears that dripped off her chin.

Primrose barged into the room, the door slamming against the wall and denting the plaster. "What are you doing to her? I can hear her sobbing out there. Leave her alone." She dashed to Dahlia and wrapped her arms around her.

"It's okay. They're doing nothing wrong," Dahlia said in between sobs. "I keep getting upset thinking about Briar."

"Briar wouldn't want you crying over everyone and embarrassing yourself. You always claim you set an example for us, but what kind of example is this? You're a blubbering mess."

She sniffed up tears. "True. Sorry. I'm in shock."

Primrose thumped her sister's back. "Briar always said you were an ugly crier. She wouldn't want you getting puffy eyes and a blotchy face, would she?"

Dahlia looked up at Primrose, but was unable to stop the tears from falling. "I'm trying! I can't believe this is happening, though."

As Primrose kept chiding her weeping sister, I noted their similarities. Primrose was thinner with a narrower face and fuller lips. Her skin was also streaked with different colors of powdered paint, as was her white cropped T-shirt.

"We didn't mean to upset Dahlia," Finn said gently. "But we need to find out Briar's movements. It'll help us figure out who did this to her."

Primrose glared at him. "Go talk to the vampires. It's got to be one of them."

"Any information either of you could give us would be helpful."

"You've spoken to Dahlia enough. And she wouldn't keep anything from you. She's always so honest." Primrose sniffed and swiped tears off Dahlia's face with her fingers. "It's annoying, but that's my sister. Always setting a good example."

"Dahlia has been very helpful," Finn said. "If you could spare us a few minutes, we'd appreciate it."

"Me! I haven't got anything to tell you. I was having fun, while Briar was off doing whatever she wanted as usual. She only ever thinks of herself."

"Did you see her talking to anyone in particular at the festival?" Finn said. "Or was anyone bothering her or causing her trouble?"

"I didn't see her hanging out with any shady vampires, if that's what you're asking. But it wouldn't surprise me if she met one or two. She was obsessed with them. You should see her bedroom. It's like a teenage explosion of vampire envy. She's got pictures of vamps all over her walls. You'd think she was twelve, not twenty-five."

"She was that into her vampires?" Zandra said.

"It was sad. That was the only reason we were here. Briar begged for weeks for Dahlia to buy us tickets. She even refused to eat until she knew we were coming. Such a drama queen."

Dahlia snuffled up more tears and nodded. "I wasn't keen on coming to the event. Briar is so full of life, though, and loves things like this. Well, she was, and she did. She used to get so overexcited and it always drew attention. It made me worry about her standing out in a crowd and getting noticed by the wrong person."

"And you were right to worry, since that's what has happened," Primrose said. "Briar let her fantasy of hanging out with a vampire mess with her head. She must have allowed one of them to take her to the woods. Maybe he promised he'd turn her and make her immortal. That's what she wanted. She wasn't happy with boring plant power. She wanted more. She was always chasing the next big thing. Whether it was a fashion trend or a new boyfriend. Briar was a desperate loser, always trying to fit in with the trendy crowd."

I detected more than a hint of jealousy in Primrose's words. "Were you two close?"

"Of course. She was my sister. I loved her, but she was still annoying. She dragged her new boyfriend here, too. Trent said a dozen times this wasn't his thing. Of course, Briar wouldn't listen. What she wanted, she got."

"I doubt she'd have wanted this as an ending to her life," I murmured.

Primrose's eyes narrowed. "She was a nuisance, but I never wanted her dead. I liked spending time with her."

Dahlia dried her eyes on her sleeve. "You did bicker. I was always breaking you apart when you fought."

Primrose glanced at Finn. "Oh, hush. We never fought. Come on, we're leaving." She tugged Dahlia to her feet. "You don't know what you're saying because you're upset."

"One more minute. Could you tell me where you were when you learned about what happened to Briar?" Finn said to Primrose.

Primrose's eyebrows shot up. "I wasn't involved. Look at my teeth. I'm not a vampire. I'm your basic green-fingered witch." She flashed her neat white teeth at him. "If I bit anyone with these, I wouldn't even leave a mark."

"It's not that we consider you a suspect, but we need an overview of everyone's movements. You may have seen something or heard something that could be useful. Even if you think it's insignificant, it could help."

Primrose sighed. "Look at me! I was partying with the environmental lot at the second color dash. And I was running around with my top off to let the girls breathe. And since I'm well endowed, and these babies are natural, I was getting plenty of attention. Ask any of the guys who were there, and they'll confirm they saw me. I only stopped partying because Dahlia found me and said something had happened."

Finn's cheeks flushed as he jotted down her comment. He behaved himself by not looking at her chest. "Perfect. Thank you."

"Let's go to the café," Primrose said to Dahlia. "I'm exhausted, and I need a shower. And I expect you're hungry. I remember when our parents died, you ate your grief for two months."

Dahlia's eyes widened a fraction. "I did not."

"Someone was eating all the chocolate chip cookies out of the pantry, and it wasn't me. And Briar was always too worried about her figure to eat junk. Come on, let's get out of here." Primrose arched a brow at Finn. "If we're allowed to go."

"Of course. I'll be in touch as soon as I have news about your sister."

They nodded, and Finn took a moment to walk them through the office.

Zandra blew out a breath. "Those ladies were intense. Primrose walked all over Dahlia, even though she's supposed to be in charge."

"Dahlia must have had her hands full raising them," I said. "And it's no surprise they went a little wild without a steadying adult influence around."

Zandra stretched out her legs. "Shall we look at the body again before we leave?"

"No! You need to sleep. We'll deal with the corpse and the dubious alibis we're uncovering tomorrow."

Chapter 7

Rude awakening

I opened one eye as something scurried across the basement floor. My other eye opened, and I looked around the gloomy interior. There were two small windows in the basement, covered by light blocking blinds, but there were a few cracks of light getting in, revealing it wasn't much past dawn.

I stayed still and listened. The scurrying stopped. I shuffled to the edge of the bed. Perhaps Sage had come in. She could have floated down the stairs in her harness, but I didn't hear the distinctive wheel squeak that went with her whenever she moved.

I peeped over the edge of the bed and came face-to-face with Archie. I made an involuntary hiss and jerked my head back, my fur fluffing.

He gently whined, but remained out of sight. "It's only me."

I gulped down my panic. Coming face-to-face with a giant hellhound while half-asleep wasn't something you ever wanted to do. I crept back to the edge of the bed. "What are you doing here?"

"I need help." Archie whined again.

"How are you even in here? Did Vorana let you inside?"

"I magicked my way in. I've got skills. And I needed to see a friend."

"Friends don't break into other friends' households and disturb them while they're sleeping. Not when they didn't get home until after one in the morning because they were questioning murder suspects." I glanced over my shoulder. "And keep it down. Zandra is asleep."

"Not anymore, I'm not," she mumbled. "Who is it?"

"You're awake!" Archie leapt onto the bed, landing so hard, he bounced me off the mattress. I flipped into the air, not having a tail to help me keep my balance, and crashed to the floor in an undignified heap.

Zandra groaned. "Archie! Get your giant paw off my stomach."

I jumped back on the bed, shook out my fur, and whacked Archie several times with a murder mitten. "Manners! You don't jump on the bed uninvited. And stop standing on my witch." I thumped him again.

He whined, and the sound was so pitiful, it pierced my heart and faded my anger. I stalked to his giant head and pushed him until he stepped off Zandra. "That's better. Now, calm yourself, and tell us what's wrong."

"But keep it simple. I wasn't ready to wake up and I'm uncaffeinated." Zandra struggled up in bed and ran her hands through her hair.

"It's Remus. He's lost his favorite handkerchief, been accused of murder, and his Blood Moon Festival has been ruined. I've tried everything, and I can't get him to smile. He's broken, and I can't fix him. I'm a useless hellhound."

"Of course, you're worried about your vampire," I said. "It's only natural. I'd be worried about my witch if she was in a similar predicament. Well, she has been, so I remember how difficult this is. But you aren't useless. You're valuable to Remus."

"But I don't know what to do. Ever since that body was found in the woods, Remus has been pacing the mansion and talking to himself. I've tried being cute, sad, goofy, but he barely notices me. I'm no good to him."

"Don't take it personally. Remus has a lot on his mind," Zandra said.

I settled on her lap to make sure Archie didn't get too close again and step on her. "The initial evidence suggests a vampire drained Briar. And since Remus keeps a watchful eye out to stop rogue vampires entering the area, it means it was one of his hive. That must be concerning him."

Archie shook his head. "It's not anyone from the hive. They're all amazing vampires. They always tell me I'm such a good boy. They give me treats and pets. None of them have tried to bite me since I joined the household."

"Because Remus ordered them not to," I said. "Not because you wouldn't make a tasty snack."

Archie growled. "They could try to snack on me, but I'd make them into a snack before they made me one. Even though vampire would taste gross,

I'd chomp, chew, and grind until there was nothing left."

I smiled at my fluffy, growling friend. I had no doubt Archie was a match for the vampires if they ever turned on him. "If it's any consolation to Remus, he's not the only suspect. Finn interviewed Briar's sisters last night."

Archie wagged his tail. "Did one of them confess?"

"No, but we need to check their alibis."

"Primrose was the only one with a decent alibi," Zandra said. "It'll be easy to learn if a busty, topless woman streaked through the color dash. Dahlia was on her own."

"Someone must have seen her," I said. "But that's our mission today. Figure out if either sister did it. If one of them is guilty, Remus and the hive are off the hook."

"Are Briar's sisters vampires?" Archie asked.

I nudged him off the bed. "Average botanical witches. Let's grab an early breakfast. My witch needs her coffee."

"What your witch needs is a few more hours in bed, but that's not happening. Give me five minutes. I'll meet you up there." Zandra rolled out of bed and headed to the bathroom.

I inhaled deeply as I arrived at the top of the staircase with Archie, happy to smell fresh coffee and toast. Vorana was an early riser.

"Morning! Oh, and Archie is here, too. With Remus?" Vorana glanced over her shoulder, but kept her back to us as she stood at the stove.

"Just me," Archie said. "I needed some advice, and I knew Juno would help me. She's so clever."

"You're too kind," I murmured.

Sage was by the door leading into the yard, and she had her hackles raised. Usually, she was the first at the breakfast table, waiting for her food, so I swiftly realized all was not well.

I trotted over and gave her a friendly head-butt. "What's up?"

When she looked at me, I stepped back. There was thunderous hatred burning in her eyes. "Haven't you seen it?"

I flicked both ears. "What am I supposed to have seen?"

"Look at her!" Sage jerked her head in Vorana's direction.

I turned at the same time as Vorana. She had a papoose wrapped around her middle. And inside that papoose sat a contented looking Ember Dreamscape, his black and white fluff poking out and his green eyes sleepily blinking.

My jaw dropped. "What's he doing here?"

Vorana grinned and gently tickled Ember's head. "I found this poor baby abandoned and alone. He was soaking wet and so pitiful that I couldn't leave him outside."

"But... But..." I looked at Sage and then back to Ember, who had a self-satisfied, smug smile on his adorable kitten face.

"You don't mind a guest staying, do you, Juno?" Vorana set mugs and plates on the table. "I'm getting him warm and fed while we find his owner. He must belong to someone. No one would ever willingly abandon such a sweet angel."

"But hasn't he told... Ouch!" I reared back as Sage scraped her claws down my side.

She nipped my ear. "Come with me. We're going outside for an emergency meeting."

"You're being odd today, Sage," Archie said. "I hope you don't have a bladder infection again. You were like this when you had crystals in your—"

"It's not my bladder! I must get outside." She scraped a paw down the door and yowled.

Vorana hurried over and opened the back door that led into the yard. Sage charged out first, and I followed her with Archie beside me, looking puzzled.

"What's going on?" Archie whispered. "Sage is scaring me."

Sage turned and faced us, waiting until the door was closed before speaking. "That little sneak showed up on the doorstep, faking being abandoned. You know what my witch is like. The second she saw him, she fell in love and brought him inside."

"Why didn't you tell her who he was as soon as he arrived?" I asked.

"Who is he?" Archie said.

"Sage's replacement. You were on that cruise with Remus when Sage got it into her head that she should retire. She found Ember to replace her, but then changed her mind and sent him packing."

"That's close enough to the truth," Sage said. "I trialed Ember as Vorana's new familiar, but then decided it wouldn't work. He was too young and excitable to be relied upon."

"And let's not forget, Vorana already has the perfect familiar," I said.

Sage grumbled cuss words under her breath. "Anyway, I sent him back to the academy and thought that was the end of it. Then he showed up with this lie about being unwanted."

"Why didn't you call him out?" I asked.

"I did! The second Vorana left us alone, I confronted him."

"He wouldn't leave?"

"Ember said he was perfect for Vorana and he'd found the right witch for him. It was my tough luck if I wouldn't accept it." Sage snorted, stamping her front paws and rattling her harness.

"You should have boxed him around his presumptuous fluffy ears and kicked him out," I said.

"How would I have explained that to Vorana? I can't look like the bad cat in this situation. She'd never forgive me if I kicked out a fake abandoned kitten. I'd look like a monster."

"Then tell her the truth," I said.

Sage heaved out a sigh and lowered her head. "What if she decides Ember is the right familiar for her? She may kick me out."

"You dope! Vorana adores you with every fiber of her being. She'd never do that to you. And even if, in some weird turn of events, she wanted to replace you with Ember, she'd keep you around, so you could live in the absolute lap of luxury."

"Ember could turn Vorana against me," Sage whispered. "He's sneaky. The fact he's shown up lying about what happened to him reveals I can't trust him. He could worm his way into Vorana's confidence and plant lies in her head about me."

"If you really believe that about your witch, then you don't know her. Vorana has a heart of gold and it's full of love for you." I patted my friend's side.

Archie attempted to lick Sage's head, but her growl made him back up.

"This is my fault. I should have said something the second Ember arrived, but I was so shocked. And now, Vorana will be angry with me for getting her a replacement without asking her first."

"That would have been sensible, but we're beyond that stage in this complication," I said.

"He seems like a cute little guy," Archie said. "Can't you share Vorana with him?"

"I am not sharing her with that creepy little kitten. I told him things wouldn't work out, but he won't accept it. It's unnatural. There's something wrong with him."

"You may be a touch biased," I murmured. Ember had been over enthusiastic and scatter brained when we'd met, but that kitten had skills. "What are you going to do?"

"Figure out a way to get rid of him without making Vorana suspicious. I have to convince him to leave."

"Maybe give it a few days and see how he fits in," Archie said. "It took me ages to get used to living in a vampire hive, but now, I love it. And I like all the vampires. You might appreciate Ember if you get to know him better."

Sage stamped a paw. "He's a sneaky little creep, and he's not staying."

Vorana opened the back door. "Are you all ready for breakfast? I have sausage patties."

We stayed silent as we headed inside, but Sage kept glaring at Ember, who was faking being asleep in the papoose. I was sympathetic about my friend's dilemma, but she had brought it on herself by introducing him to the household. Vorana's home was amazing, and she served the best food. I just hoped Sage found a way to compromise. Now Ember had his fluffy paw in the door, he looked like he wasn't leaving.

After breakfast, Archie returned to Remus, hoping to make him smile with news of the other suspects, and I walked to Angel Force with Zandra. It was the weekend, so we had a couple of days off and didn't need to worry about work. Which was handy, because we had to focus on this murder investigation and making sure Remus and his vampires were in the clear.

Finn was at his desk when we walked in. He got a coffee for Zandra and water for me, and we settled around his desk.

"Any news overnight?" I sat on a pile of crinkly paper that felt delicious under my toe beans.

"I've done some research on Briar. She has a privileged background. Everything Dahlia told us in the interview was true. They lost their parents and were left with a fortune and a huge house. Dahlia had turned eighteen the week before their parents died, so she could look after Primrose and Briar without involving social services."

"That's hardly the gift you want for your eighteenth birthday," Zandra said.

"From the information I found, there were struggles." Finn opened a screen on his computer. "Briar had a few scrapes with law enforcement. Nothing serious, but there are records of shoplifting and one for causing public disorder."

"What about Primrose?" I asked.

"No criminal activity, but she was expelled from three schools after her parents died for misuse of magic. She went off the rails."

"It's no surprise. Their world got knocked off its axis after their parents' untimely death," I said.

"Anything about Dahlia?" Zandra said.

"She had a full scholarship to the Academy of Witch Art and Design. She'd received several awards and won competitions for her paintings using plant dyes. But she gave it up to look after her sisters."

"Couldn't she have done both?" I asked.

"Doubtful. Dahlia would have had to move across the country to attend the academy. She couldn't have taken her sisters with her."

"That must have been hard on her," I said. "It could have left lingering resentment."

"It's a possible motive," Finn said. "But why act on that resentment now?"

"It could have grown," I said. "Dahlia gave up her dream to look after her sisters, and then Briar repaid her by breaking the law, becoming a vampire obsessed party girl, and disrespecting her. Maybe she'd had enough. She saw Briar doing something that angered her and confronted her. This was the result."

"That doesn't explain the bite mark on Briar's neck," Zandra said. "Primrose and Dahlia are witches, not vampires. If either sister was involved, how did they make those holes and drain her so efficiently?"

I nodded. "The ground around Briar had no blood spatter on it. Maybe she was killed somewhere else and her body left in the woods. Has anyone reported finding a kill site?"

"No. And the area was searched for anything like that. But with everyone traipsing around, not to mention the color dashes that literally encourage people to run and dance as far and as fast as they can, any clues would have been destroyed." Finn sat back. "I don't see the sisters as prime suspects. Although the girls were raised chaotically, I'm not sure they have strong motives for murdering Briar."

"Until we've checked both their alibis, they stay on the list," I said.

"I agree." Finn looked around. "Cythera is at a meeting if you want to look at the body. The examination took place first thing, so Briar is still on a gurney."

"It's what I live for, to see dead bodies," I said. "Take as to the corpse."

Zandra shook her head as she reluctantly peeled herself out of the chair.

Finn led us through the building to the small morgue. It was a stark, sterile space, with stainless steel tables and gleaming equipment set out neatly. The air was heavy with the scent of antiseptic and formaldehyde, and my booping snooter detected a faint undertone of decay. That must be Briar.

Finn took us to a gurney at the back of the room. With a small amount of reluctance in my paws, I followed him, and waited as he removed the sheet covering Briar.

"Anything unusual found other than the bite marks on the neck?" I hopped onto the end of the gurney, taking extra care because my balance wasn't at its best while my tail was missing.

"No other injuries, incisions, or concerning marks." Finn consulted a chart. "The cause of death is listed as exsanguination by bite. Not listed as a vampire bite and drain, though. At least, not yet. But that's the direction Cythera is going."

"I understand why." I picked my way carefully along the gurney, avoiding treading on any chilled pieces of flesh.

"Take a closer look at the holes in her neck," Finn said. "Tell me what you think."

"I'll stay here and look from a distance," Zandra said. "I'm not great with the stiffs."

Neither was I, but there were often interesting things to discover when you looked with a dispassionate eye and forced yourself not to think of the person as a person, but as a puzzle to put together. Once you had those pieces in the right order, you could dispense justice.

After a moment of inspection, I looked up. "The holes are ragged around the edges. An experienced vampire would make two small, round holes. Simple puncture wounds straight in the jugular vein."

"The examination suggests there were several attempts at making those holes," Finn said.

"Briar struggled," Zandra said. "When she realized what the vampire wanted, she fought back. He kept trying to sink in his fangs, but missed."

"There is no bruising on her arms or face to suggest she was held," Finn said. "No signs of a fight."

Zandra shrugged. "He compelled her to stay still."

"So why the messy holes if she didn't move?"

"Was there blood spatter down her clothing or on her torso?" I said. "I don't recall seeing any when we found her in the woods."

"Nothing like that," Finn said. "It was a clean drain. Which is odd, because the holes look like a new vampire made them. First-time feeders are messy. They get overexcited and the end result is gory. But this is a clean kill. There wasn't a drop of blood on Briar's clothing or skin, other than a small amount around the holes, which is standard."

"Maybe more than one vampire was involved. One newbie who couldn't get it right, so his more experienced friend took over and showed him how it was done," Zandra said.

"Or it wasn't vampires," I said. "We know Remus runs a tight ship. Well, hive. He'd never let his vampires run rogue."

"Something definitely bit and drained Briar." Finn set down the chart and approached the door. "I'm heading back to the campsite this morning to ask around, see if any of the festival goers or protestors saw anything that could help. Want to join me?"

"I can think of no better way to spend my weekend than questioning people about a mysterious murder." I hopped off the gurney.

"I can think of about a thousand better things we could do," Zandra said. "Sleeping in, having a lazy breakfast, going for a walk in the woods—"

"And finding another body drained?" I shook my head. "The fun comes later. Let's return to the murder scene and see who's been draining our visitors."

Chapter 8

A worrying fang

"It looks like no one has left." I trotted ahead of Zandra as we headed toward the busy makeshift campsite that had grown overnight outside Remus's mansion. The food stalls were still selling goodies, and people were milling about, not seeming sure what to do next.

"Cythera must have insisted they cancel the event." Zandra dodged a man wearing a feathered hat and stick on glittery wings. "There'd be no way she'd allow the festival to continue after what happened."

"If she has issued that order, everyone must be ignoring her." I looked up at my witch. "We often do."

Zandra smirked. "Where should we start? There are so many people that the thought of tackling them all makes me want to head back to bed."

Finn looked around. "It's definitely busier than I thought it would be. A murder hasn't put people off of coming. There should be more angels arriving soon to help with the information gathering. We'll wait for them."

"And we'll have treats while we wait. Once we're fueled up, you'll be more inclined to work." I saw Edith's brownie stand and walked over, Zandra behind me, muttering and glaring at the glittery strangers and colorfully dressed festival attendees. She fell quiet when we got within sniffing distance of the delicious treats. I knew my witch, and she could never resist a delicious, warm, gooey, chocolaty splurge.

We waited several minutes with Finn for the queue to move, giving Zandra time to examine the handwritten board, which tempted people with caramel pecan triple chocolate delights, mocha maple surprise, and strawberry cream brownie dream. They sounded delicious, even though I was more of a savory fan.

Zandra read through the list of treats several times. "I can't decide what to have. They all sound amazing."

"Get one of everything," I said.

Finn chuckled. "That won't fuel you. That'll give you a sugar coma. No fun."

She tilted her head. "This is the magic brownie stand, right?"

I nodded.

"I don't want to float off the ground while talking to witnesses. I need to keep a clear head."

We stepped up to the counter.

"If you need a pep in your step, I've got just the thing, deary." Edith smiled at us and lifted a tray of red velvet brownies studded with dark chocolate chunks.

"Perfect. My witch will have two," I said.

"One. And a small one," Zandra said. "We're working, remember?"

"One small yummy treat full of magical goodness coming up. Anything for you, cutie?" Edith winked at me as she speared the red velvet brownie and shook sweet smelling pink icing sugar over it.

"Have you got anything with salmon?"

She wrinkled her nose. "Not much call for salmon and chocolate."

"Then, I'll pass."

"And you?" Edith looked at Finn.

"Anything coffee flavored."

"I've got just the thing. What do you all do for work?" Edith placed the brownies on paper plates and handed them over.

"Finn's with Angel Force. We freelance for them on their trickiest cases. We're their renowned experts," I said.

Finn grinned as he took his brownie and bit into it.

Zandra shot me a warning look. "We kind of do that. We're investigating what happened to the woman who died here last night. Did you know her?"

"Oh, that poor young woman. She was the life and soul of the party. So sad." Edith rested a hand over her heart. "I always look out for the butterflies at these events, but that one escaped me."

"Butterflies?" I asked.

"The beauties that attract the most attention at festivals. But I was so busy, I couldn't see straight. Next thing I know, she's gone." Her jaw wobbled, suggesting tears were close.

I flicked an ear. "Had you met Briar before this festival?"

"No. But I saw her at the café. Briar stood out from the crowd. She was so pretty."

"I saw her there, too. And when you offered her a brownie when she arrived at the festival, she was rude to you."

Edith puckered her mouth. "Yes, a little. I didn't mind, though. It was high spirits. Young people can get overexcited and forget themselves."

"I'd mind if someone was rude to me." Zandra nibbled the edge of her brownie. "Wow! This is great."

"Thank you. My brownies are always popular. It's just so sad things may have to stop before they get started." Edith leaned across the counter. "I'm not even sure the vampires got to celebrate their Blood Moon."

"They didn't. Not in the way they wanted." I glanced over my shoulder at the growing queue of hungry, shuffling people. "Are you sure you didn't mind Briar being rude to you?"

Edith set down the tray of brownies and shrugged. "I may have been annoyed. After all, manners cost nothing. But I've learned to deal with headstrong young people. My boy, Drayton, has a stubborn streak bigger than this mansion, yet we always find a way to compromise. I'm sure she meant no harm."

"Perhaps Briar forgot her manners once too often," Zandra said. "Did you see anyone arguing with her?"

Edith furrowed her brow, then nodded. "She enjoyed the drama."

"Hey, Edith. What's the hold-up?" a guy three spaces back in the queue called out. "I need my mocha triple brownie delight."

"Nothing, lovey. I won't be a moment."

The guy slid out of the line and strode toward us. I recognized his distinctive style of dress, with a long black cape brushing the back of his knees, and a scraggly beard down to his pecs. He was a member of Gaian's gang.

He stopped by the counter. "What gives? Are these three bothering you?"

Edith smiled and shook her head. "Not for a second. They're doing important work for Angel Force, and investigating what happened to that girl. I was just telling them what I know. You can wait a few minutes, can't you?"

He huffed out a grunt. "I don't want you bothered."

Edith patted his cheek. "You're so sweet. This is Tirel. He's been my guardian angel since I got here."

"You're in Gaian's gang," I said to him.

"That's right. And I've seen you around, too. You used to be friends with Sorcha."

"As far as I'm aware, we still are." Zandra brushed crumbs off her fingers and folded her arms across her chest.

Tirel scowled at her. "Gaian doesn't think you're good for her. Stay away from the café."

Zandra drew herself up to her not massive height and stepped closer to Tirel. "You're telling me where I should go in my own town?"

I fluffed my fur, desperately missing my huge white tail that always looked splendid when fully floofed, and hissed.

Edith bustled around the counter, "Now, now! There's no need for that. No fighting. You don't want to scare my customers away. Tirel, take this brownie and get out of here."

"I'm staying until they go." He grabbed the brownie. "They're troublemakers."

"Says who? Your leader?" Zandra said. "The only trouble around here has happened since your gang came to town."

His top lip curled. "You ain't seen nothing yet."

"What does that mean?"

"Ignore Tirel. He's all bluster and no bite." Edith's hand fluttered against her chest. "And he's been a sweetheart to me. He helped me when I was struggling with some boxes and carried them to my tent. I didn't get here early enough to get a good spot to camp, so I'm by the trees. It's a long walk when your knees ache and your back protests."

"You should move from there. It's not safe after what happened," Tirel said. "I can help you move."

"You're such a good boy. You remind me of my son."

A flush of pleasure lit Tirel's bristled cheeks.

"Tirel walked me through the woods when we heard someone had been hurt," Edith said. "I was glad of his company when I learned how serious it was."

Tirel nodded. "I wouldn't let you struggle alone. It's not right."

"You see! He's a lovely young man. Not a fighter." Edith glanced at the growing queue. "As for that unfortunate young lady, she enjoyed a fight. She bickered with the women she came with. I assumed they were sisters because they looked similar."

I kept an eye on Tirel as I turned my attention to Edith. "What did they fight about?"

"They were getting treats from my stand when Briar called one of them a hefty cow! The poor girl was almost in tears."

"Which sister did she insult?" I said. "The one with the glasses?"

"That's right. She had big, round glasses. The poor thing stepped away from the queue and pretended to clean them, but I could see she was stopping tears. And later, I saw Briar getting into a fight with two men. She was encouraging them to fight over her." Edith shook her head. "And then there was the vampire who got mean with her."

"Briar argued with a vampire?" Finn asked. "Which one?"

"The flamboyant one. The one with the crimson and pink top hat. He was hard to miss."

Zandra glanced down at me. There was only one vampire in this area who wore top hats.

"What was his name?" Zandra said.

"I don't know the vampires around here. I think it's the one who owns the big house. He seemed in charge, anyway."

"Did you hear what they fought about?" I asked.

"No, I wasn't close to them when they argued. I was collecting supplies from my storage tent. All suppliers have them beside the main house. Briar was hurrying along beside the vampire and talking to him, but he was ignoring her. At least, he tried to, but she grabbed his arm and wouldn't let go."

"What did he do?" I said.

"He spoke to her, and I could see he was unhappy, but she didn't give up and kept following him. She even shoved him in the back to get his attention. That was when he turned on her."

I sucked in a breath. "And then what?"

"Briar hit him! She thumped his chest several times. The vampire shoved her away and walked off."

I let out the breath. Remus lied to us about knowing Briar.

"I'm so sorry. I wish I could talk more, but the queue is getting large." Edith gestured at the grumpy people behind us.

"I've served behind a bar, so I can handle dishing out brownies." Tirel strode behind the counter and wrapped a spare white apron around his middle. "Who's next?"

Edith beamed at him. "You're so adorable. I'm tempted to adopt you." She looked at us. "I hope I've been helpful. You know where I am when you want more treats."

"Thanks. You've been more helpful than you know." I walked away from the stand with Zandra and Finn.

None of us spoke for several minutes, but we were headed toward the mansion.

"This makes no sense," Zandra said. "Edith must have been talking about Remus."

I nodded. "And we need to ask him why he lied to us."

Remus was easy to find. Although he tolerated daylight, he usually stayed inside when it was bright, and we discovered him reclining on a chaise lounge, with a book in his hand, his eyes half-closed.

"Greetings, Remus, we need to talk." I stalked over to him.

"Good morning, my tailless beauty. What brings you here so early?"

"One guess." Zandra put her hands on her hips. "You lied. You were seen fighting with Briar."

Remus froze, then slowly blinked. "Is it raining yet?"

Finn glanced at the window. "No. What's that got to do with Briar?"

"I need air. Let's go outside. I can smell rain coming, so it'll soon be cloudy. Besides, Archie needs some exercise."

Archie appeared in the doorway, wagging his tail. "Did someone say it was walk time? Hey everyone! You here to help Remus clear his name and catch the bad guy?"

"Something like that." I just hoped Remus didn't turn out to be the bad guy, or Archie's heart would break.

"Let's go out the back way, so we don't need to mingle with the great unwashed. And that's where my angel guards are lurking. They'll have to come along, too, but they won't cause trouble.

They're sweet, but poor conversationalists. Shall we?" Remus stood and gestured to the door.

We walked into the hallway, and he led us along a luxurious corridor adorned with velvet cream wallpaper and out of a back door. We headed along a gravel path, shaded by weeping willows. Archie bounded ahead, oblivious to the awkward conversation that was about to take place.

Only when we were in the shadow of more trees did Remus look at us, a hint of shame on his face. "I confess that I argued with Briar on the night she died."

Archie stumbled over his paws and turned to face Remus. "You did? I didn't know. When?"

"Patience, my hound. All will be revealed." He threw a stick for Archie.

"Go on," I said. "What were you arguing about?"

"Briar discovered I was running the Blood Moon Festival and sought me out. The foolish child asked me to turn her on the spot." He snorted gently. "She had no idea how difficult turning someone is, and how long it takes to choose suitable individuals to make into vampires. She assumed I'd tip her back like the movie vampires, plunge my fangs into her neck, and that would be it. She'd be immortal forever."

"Briar didn't take it well when you told her no?" I asked.

Remus shrank into himself. "She was awful. And she yelled! She told me I wasn't a real vampire, and I wasn't even a man. Which, of course, I'm not. I'm so much more. I'm immortal. Eternal. Magnificent."

"And egotistical," I said.

"When you've seen as much as I have and lived to tell the tale, your ego will be just as emboldened."

I didn't comment. I'd certainly seen interesting things during my tenure as a demigoddess.

"Why conceal the fight from us?" Finn said. "You must have known someone would see you."

"I didn't. And the fight was over in a matter of minutes. Barely that. I forgot about it. To me, it was insignificant."

"Remus! You must have known this would make you a suspect," I said.

He lifted his shoulders. "Perhaps. And I realize it looks bad. But just because we argued, doesn't mean I killed her. And Briar wasn't the only one who begged to be turned that night. There were dozens of willing apprentices who tried to convince me they should become a part of my hive. They're all still alive. Even though they don't want to be."

"Is that how Briar got hold of your handkerchief?" Zandra said.

"I assume so. She was clutching at me with her cold little hands. She could have taken it without me noticing." Remus stopped walking and looked over to where the angels were lurking close by. "I promise you, I'm innocent."

"Maybe so, but Cythera will find out about this fight. She'll think you did it," I said.

"I'm certain of that." Remus clasped his hands together. "You will still help me, won't you? I am sorry for hiding this, but it means nothing."

Archie raced back with the stick and dropped it at Remus's feet.

"Of course we'll still help," I said. "We know you didn't do this. But you can't keep things from us."

Finn nodded. "If Cythera had found out about this before we did, you'd be in a cell."

Remus sighed, then turned and continued walking. "This is such a puzzle. I've spoken to all of my vampires and they promised me they didn't do this. They don't lie to me. Most of them can't because it makes them unwell."

"Do you have any recently turned vampires staying here?" I said. "Any who would make a mess of biting someone?"

"No. We've been waiting for the festival before introducing anyone new. The plan was to have twenty-four baby vampires to look after. Now, I have none. We're so disappointed." He lifted one eyebrow. "Why do you ask about newly turned vampires?"

"The bite holes in Briar's neck were untidy," I said. "I wondered if a new recruit had lost control."

"My hive is full of skilled hunters. We never make a mistake." A benign smile slid across Remus's face. "And there are no rogue vampires around. The angels need to reconsider which creature did this."

"Given the evidence, Cythera is set on finding a vampire for this crime," Finn said.

"That's even more disappointing news." Remus threw the stick for Archie again. "Is there any positive progress with the investigation?"

I hopped over a muddy hole. "Fortunately for you, you're not the only suspect Angel Force is interested in."

"The only vampire, though?"

I nodded.

"I'll help in any way I can," Remus said. "I want this matter dealt with. And I still have hope we can pull together a festival. As you can see from the growing crowd, people are keen on celebrating the blood moon. We still have tonight, even though its intensity will have dimmed."

"Cythera will have a thing or two to say about that," Zandra said.

Finn hummed under his breath, his expression rueful.

Remus stopped at the top of a small hill and looked out. It was an impressive view, showing Crimson Cove in the distance. But my attention wasn't on the view. It was on the symbols painted on a slab of rock.

My pulse quickened as I inspected them. "Remus, how long have these been here?"

He turned toward me and his forehead furrowed. "I've no idea. I've never seen them before. Did a festival attendee make them? There's all that powdered paint around from the color dashes. Have you been through a color dash yet? They're most amusing."

"Not with my white fur. And I don't think these symbols have anything to do with that." I walked around the rock and found more symbols on the other side. Similar white splodges set in a circle.

"What's got you so interested?" Zandra said. "Someone who ate a magic brownie probably painted them. I'm buzzy after Edith's treat, so I'm glad I only had one. I'd probably be hallucinating squiggles if I had anymore."

Before I could explain, the flap of wings overhead drew my attention. Cythera arrived, planting one fist on the ground as she landed superhero style. She stood and shook her wings back into place.

She ignored me and Zandra. "Remus, I have more questions for you."

"Maybe she's found out about the fight," Zandra whispered to me. "This could mean trouble for Remus."

I nodded, but my attention was still on the symbols. Whoever was leaving these had spread their net.

Archie hurried over and knocked his head against my side, almost sending me tumbling into the dirt. "Juno! The angels! You must go with Remus and stop them mistreating him."

"We never mistreat suspects." Cythera sent a caustic glare at Archie, making him whimper.

"It's just questions. He'll be okay," I said.

"They'll lock him up and I'll never see him again." Archie whined some more. "Juno, please. You said you'd help."

I looked back at the symbols. I wanted to investigate them, but there was no time. Remus needed me. But I'd be back. These symbols were spreading, and that meant trouble.

Chapter 9

Missing people

Remus was once again seated in an interview room at Angel Force. Cythera and Finn were conducting the interview, but this time, I'd been allowed into the room with Zandra. Archie was also there, tucked in one corner, and Cythera had made him promise not to make a sound or jump up on anyone.

"From the sullen look on your face, my dearest angel friend, it suggests you've learned something that displeases you." Remus rested his manicured hands on the table. "What nefarious deeds from my past have you uncovered that are making you look like you're chewing a thorny wasp with an everlasting sting?"

Cythera placed six files in front of her. "I've been looking into missing persons cases. These people were last seen around Oak Park Ridge. Then they vanished."

"That's unfortunate," Remus said smoothly. "We have dangerous animals in the woods. If someone isn't from around here, they could find themselves in trouble."

"Some would say you're a dangerous animal." Cythera opened a file and took out a sheet of paper. "Do these names sound familiar to you?" She read off six names. All male.

Remus gently patted his hair. "I meet so many people, it's hard to say for certain. As you know, I often open my home for social gatherings. You're always invited, but you rarely attend. Your presence is missed."

"Remus! Take this seriously."

The glimmer of amusement faded from his eyes. "I always take you seriously. Please, continue."

"There's a connection between these missing people. They all came to the area just before you held a Blood Moon Festival. They were never seen again."

Remus didn't speak, his gaze on the table.

"People don't vanish," Cythera said.

I gently cleared my throat. "Some magical beings do."

Cythera's wings fluttered, and she scrunched the paper.

Remus shifted his head from side to side, as if attempting to remove a tension knot in his neck. "I'll have to check my records, which are impeccably maintained. And I always submit my turning paperwork to you, so you know I've done nothing untoward to these individuals."

"You do. So it was easy to discover all these people requested to be turned by you. What happened? They're not in your hive. I know all of your vampires. What did you do to them?"

A thin, high-pitched whimper came from Archie's corner.

"Silence!" Cythera barked.

"Sorry. That didn't come out of my mouth. I toot when I'm nervous." Archie curled his tail around himself and hid his face.

I stared hard at Remus as the aromatic scent of Archie's nervous toot drifted around the room. Remus kept shifting in his seat. He was uncomfortable.

"I'm happy to show you the paperwork for those names," he finally said. "I have nothing immoral to conceal from you."

"I insist on seeing it. It's no coincidence the turning requests were made. They visited your Blood Moon Festival, and then they were never seen again."

"Perhaps they changed their minds."

Cythera huffed out an angry breath. "Unlikely. You're always bragging about your waiting list."

"I don't brag. It's a mere statement of fact." Remus relaxed a fraction. "Perhaps they weren't truthful on their application, and when we met, I realized I'd been deceived. I don't turn shy mice, no matter how sweet they are. They'd be a terrible fit for the hive."

"I'm well aware your hive is full of flamboyant—"

"Hunks?"

"No! Flamboyant—"

"Intelligent, dazzling creatures who love to entertain?"

Cythera ground her teeth. "Remus! Stop! Explain yourself. What happened to these people? I know you're hiding something from me. I demand answers."

Archie whined again, this time, the noise coming from his mouth, but a glare from Cythera silenced him.

"I... I have an explanation. It may not be one you want to hear, though," Remus said.

Cythera inhaled sharply. "I'm listening."

Remus steepled his fingers together. "You must understand, turning someone into a vampire is complicated."

"I do understand. What did you do to them? You turned them but lost control?"

"Never! I'm a responsible master."

Cythera tilted her head at the same time as me and Zandra. "You did turn them?"

"In a way."

Cythera jabbed a finger on the sheet of paper. "These aren't members of your hive."

"Not officially."

Doubt flickered through me as Remus stumbled over his words. What was he hiding?

There was a tense pause, punctuated by nervous toots that fired out of Archie's rear end.

"Did you drain them and hide their bodies? Just like you did to Briar?" Cythera asked.

Everyone seemed to hold their breath as they waited for the answer. It was also a handy technique to avoid inhaling too many of Archie's toots.

Remus held his fingers under his nose. "I'd never do such a despicable thing. I have the answers you need at my home. Let's return there and have tea and polite conversation."

Cythera flicked a glance at Finn. "I don't want tea."

"Are you sure? I have Earl Grey. Your favorite." Remus tried for a smile, but it wavered. He was worried, which only made my alarm grow. Maybe our vampire friend wasn't so innocent, after all.

Half an hour later, and after some gentle persuasion by Finn and the promise of fancy cakes from France by Remus, we were back at his mansion. Cythera was settled at his desk, while we remained on a comfortable red velvet couch with plump, patterned feather cushions.

An early lunch had been brought for us, although Cythera refused all food, claiming she was working and couldn't afford to be distracted. Despite her protests, I'd seen her looking at the pink and yellow iced French fancies more than once.

Several of Remus's vampires lurked in the room, on the pretense of reading books, but I knew they were being nosy. And I didn't blame them, since their master was on the hook for murder.

Remus was perched on a seat next to us, his head bowed, and Archie lay across his feet. "My sincerest apologies for this confusion. I fear I've gotten myself into unexpected hot water."

"Then clear it up," I said. "What happened to those people?"

Remus closed his eyes for a second and winced. "I never let a vampire down, even if their turning doesn't go as planned."

"When a turning fails, what happens?" Zandra said. "Does the person die?"

"Now and again, there are fatalities. Those aren't the problem. Everyone knows the risks, and they all sign waivers, so we can't be charged with a crime because they weren't strong enough to make it through the change."

Cythera snorted at that comment as she perused the paperwork Remus had laid out for her.

"It's an ancient agreement made between the angels and the vampires." Remus raised his voice a fraction. "And I'm a responsible master. If anyone fails to turn and they leave family behind, I settle a sum of money on them."

"Do they always accept it?" I asked. "Some might consider it blood money."

"How appropriate a description, you quaintly pale fluffy. They never know it comes from me." Remus lifted his head, his eyes showing a rare hint of tiredness. "They receive an unexpected windfall from a distant relative, or win a prize draw they forgot they entered. I make sure anyone left behind doesn't suffer. It's more than many masters do."

I studied Remus for a moment. "I've heard of people who go through the transformation, but cannot gain control of their vampire abilities. Is that what happened here?"

Remus inhaled slowly. "Yes. And those are the individuals Cythera is concerned about."

"What's this?" Cythera lifted a sheet of paper off the desk. "I've seen several mentions of a vampire spa."

"As I was about to tell my most wonderful friends, the people you identified as missing didn't adapt to their turning." Remus gently shuffled his feet out from under Archie's furry chest, stood, and walked to the desk. Archie lumbered to his paws and followed him.

"You send them to a spa?" Cythera said.

"It's a kind of spa. More like a paradise for them. Those vampires have control issues. They get thorough training, but even if they had one-on-one supervision for decades, they'd still struggle not to attack anything warm-blooded. And I mean, anything. No creature is off limits. And my feral children are always on the hunt. They never stop, never sleep. They only want to hunt."

"I see." She set down the paper. "It is within your rights as the owner of these vampires to destroy them. But I see no paperwork to show that's what happened."

Remus hissed softly at her. "I never destroy my creations. I take responsibility for the outcome of each turning. Even if that outcome is... unfortunate."

"Those who can't get control of their powers go to your spa?" I walked over, curious to learn more about Remus's responsibilities as a vampire master. I'd met plenty of head vampires over the years, and some barely held onto a thread of humanity, and happily snapped necks and drained those who didn't obey them.

"I send them away, and they live together, so they have companionship. They're regularly checked so I know they're content. The spa, as I like to call it, is secure."

"Why was this establishment not reported to me?" Cythera said. "Unresolved missing persons cases are an issue. I should have been informed."

"Will your key performance indicators suffer because of Remus's omission?" I said.

Her lips thinned. "This is about more than my reports being incomplete."

I blinked in surprise. Cythera cared. She just liked to hide it extremely well.

"I'd like to visit this spa and make sure these individuals are thriving," she said.

Remus clasped his hands together and bowed his head. "I'd strongly advise against it. An angel visiting a colony of feral vampires would be an issue. All that sweet cinnamon angel blood drifting in the air." He smacked his lips together. "The thought of it is even making me drool."

"Don't be disgusting," Cythera said. "Did you let these feral vampires loose at the festival? Did one of them kill Briar and you're covering for them?"

"If one of them had gotten loose, you'd have had hundreds of fatalities to deal with." Anger flashed in Remus's eyes. "I'd never be so irresponsible as to let them be free on the grounds."

"Once they're in the spa, they never leave?" I asked.

"I occasionally take them on trips, but they're always shackled and sedated. It makes them easier to handle."

"That sounds harsh," Zandra said. "Are they really that dangerous?"

"It's the only way to ensure the safety of others. And some of them beg to be sedated. They find the overwhelming urge to eat too intense." Remus sighed. "It wounds my shriveled heart that I'm not always successful with my turnings, but I'm better than most masters. My feral children are no risk to anyone or themselves."

"I'd still like to arrange a visit," Cythera said.

Remus hesitated. "Let me see what I can do. And my apologies again for concealing a small amount of the truth from you."

"More than small," Zandra muttered.

Remus slid her the stink eye. "My feral vampires must consent to having their situation shared. Many of them have no desire for friends and family to know what they've become."

"Better to be considered missing than a feral?" I said.

Remus nodded. "Most of them believe so. I honor their wishes."

"Your paperwork is good enough," Cythera said. "But I'll be reporting this up the chain of command. And I'll want commentary with the Vampire Council as to whether your methods are acceptable. This feral vampire spa is odd."

"The Council agrees with me on this matter. Although some of them say I'm too soft-hearted and should do as you suggest and destroy my irregular creations." He shook his head. "Every beautiful, imperfectly perfect misfit has a place in my heart."

"Even the rabid ones who want to rip out everyone's throat?" Zandra said.

"Even them." Remus spread his hands. "Now, if I can't tempt you to an early lunch or a glass of champagne, is there anything else I can do for you, my most delightful angel?"

"No. No refreshments are required."

"Are you sure? I noticed you admiring the French fancies. Shall I have a box made up for you to take home?"

Cythera drew in a breath, suggesting she planned to continue arguing with Remus over his unique vampire spa, rather than thank him for his generous offer of treats.

I jumped onto the desk, overshooting because of my lack of tail to balance me. I stumbled on my paws and stopped in front of Cythera. "You've seen that Remus's paperwork is pristine, and he's doing his best for all of his vampires. You need to focus on the other suspects, or the killer will escape."

"What makes you think I'm not?" She shooed me away as she tidied the papers I'd scattered.

I dabbed the back of her hand with a paw. "What about Briar's sisters? Do their alibis check out? Was Primrose in the color dash with no clothes on?"

"Primrose was wearing shorts, so she wasn't naked," Cythera said. "And she was seen at the color dash. I've discounted her from the investigation."

"Excellent. So, you've eliminated one suspect. And Dahlia?"

Cythera's glare was laced with irritation. "We're having trouble getting anyone to confirm where she was. We're still looking into her alibi."

"Which means Remus isn't your only suspect. This day gets better. Dahlia has a decent motive for murder, since she may have decided she'd had enough of babysitting her siblings and saw a chance to get rid of one of them."

A lurking vampire who could have been a stand-in for a young Brad Pitt stood from his seat, but Remus held up a hand and shook his head. The vampire slunk back, not looking happy.

I studied the vampire. He looked miserable. Still ridiculously handsome, but there was something in his gaze that suggested heartbreak or misery. Had he been about to say something about the murder? I tried to catch his gaze, but he refused to look up from his surly slouch.

"If you're referring to the charming Dahlia Vixen," Remus said. "I met her at the festival. What a delightful woman. I'm sure it wasn't her. You should look elsewhere for your killer. But not here."

"Although Dahlia doesn't have a solid alibi yet, I'm not convinced the sisters are involved," Zandra said. "What about the boyfriend, Trent?"

"Yes! We heard Briar was being fought over by two men at the festival. Any news on them?" I asked.

Cythera slapped a file down on to the desk. "We're working on it! I already have a list of suspects. And Remus is still on it."

He dipped his chin and jutted out his bottom lip. "I'm most unhappy to learn that. You're sure there's nothing I can do to convince you I'm as innocent as a freshly baked apple pie?"

Cythera jabbed a finger at him. "There is nothing innocent about you. This whole situation is suspicious. The missing people turned into feral vampires you never told me about, and Briar found dead on your grounds after having been drained by a vampire. I don't like it."

"Allegedly drained by a vampire," I said.

"You're keeping secrets," Cythera said. "We'll be speaking more about Briar and these feral spa vampires."

Remus placed a hand over his heart. "It's a treat I look forward to. Perhaps, next time, you'll try the Earl Grey and the cakes."

The door blasted open and a black-haired vampire wearing dark jeans and a pristine white shirt raced into the room. "It was me! I killed Briar. Arrest me for her murder."

Chapter 10

Fanged fiend revealed

"Valentine! You didn't kill that young woman." Remus dashed to the anxious vampire, who was a spit for Rhett Butler in his prime, and clutched him by his broad shoulders. "Take back that confession. Cythera, ignore what you heard. Valentine hasn't been himself, recently."

"I'm fine." Valentine's panicked gaze flicked to Cythera. "I did it! I can't keep quiet about it anymore. I'm guilty. And it's eating me up thinking about it. Remus taught me better."

Cythera strode over and joined the vampires, and I was right behind her with Zandra. This was a curious turn of events.

Cythera's wings flared behind her in an unnecessarily showy strength display. "You're confessing to the murder of Briar Vixen?"

Valentine looked at Remus and gulped. "Yes. It was me."

"No! You're not that kind of vampire." Remus gently shook Valentine by the shoulder. "You're one of my most loyal vampires. I gave the order that no one was to be harmed at the festival, so I know you wouldn't break that command."

"I couldn't resist her. There was too much temptation. All those warm bodies and exposed skin. I had to have a taste!"

Remus appeared to struggle for air, one hand going to his stomach. "We feasted before the festival. You were so full you could barely move. I joked I'd have to roll you out because you'd eaten so much."

"I'm greedy! I'm sorry. Take me away. I'm the only one involved in this crime. Remus is innocent."

"How long have you been a vampire?" I asked Valentine.

His intense gray-blue gaze trailed down to me. "Why do you want to know?"

"It's relevant to the investigation. How long?"

"Eighty-three years. I was turned when I was thirty."

"Not a recently turned vampire, then?"

"Valentine has been with me for a long time," Remus said. "I rely on him. It's why you can't take him away."

"I can do exactly that, since he confessed," Cythera said.

"Wait a moment," I said. "Valentine, would you consider yourself an expert feeder?"

"Um... of course. Remus teaches us how to enjoy our meals but not make any mess. It's undignified to spill your food. And we always ensure those we feast on are happy." Valentine glanced at Remus. "I know some vampires care little about that sort of thing, but we're civilized. That's why I was so eager to join this hive."

"Exactly! And we don't go around munching on innocent women at festivals, do we?" Remus clutched Valentine's shoulders. "Don't do this. It won't help the situation."

"I can't keep quiet any longer. I'm sorry, Remus. I never meant to let you down." Valentine lowered his head.

"Come with me," Cythera said. "I need to question you."

"He's going nowhere." Remus blocked the door.

"Don't make this any more difficult than it already is," Cythera said. "I should take you in too, since you're his master. What's to say you didn't compel Valentine to undertake this gruesome act?"

Remus flashed his fangs. "You're wasting your time following this line of investigation. Valentine is innocent. So am I."

As Cythera and Remus bickered over who got Valentine, I backed away a few steps, nudging Zandra with my head until she did the same. I had a good idea why Valentine had crashed into the room and confessed. He was worried about Remus's innocence. But from the determined look in Cythera's eyes, she intended to pursue this line of inquiry to the bitter end.

"We'll go with Valentine," I offered. "Make sure everything is done above board."

"There's no need for you to interfere," Cythera said. "Everything is under control."

"There's every need. Valentine requires representation. It's only right he gets the best." I prodded Cythera's firm calf with my paw. "That's us, before you come back with a witty retort."

"Please, take Juno and Zandra with you," Remus said to Valentine. "You can rely on them. They always ensure justice is done."

"Then they'll only be helping to put me behind bars. It's where I belong." Valentine gripped Remus's hand. "We can't have this murder hanging over the hive. It's bad for our reputation. It's bad for you. I know what I'm doing. Perhaps you'll visit me when things settle. Bring me some treats. You know I love a silk pillow."

"If you murdered that young woman, there'll be no visits and no silk anything for you," Cythera said. "We all know what the Vampire Council does to vampires who can't control themselves."

Remus hissed. "It won't come to that. Valentine won't lose his fangs because of this farce."

"Relax," Zandra murmured to him. "Or you'll be arrested, too."

He glowered at Cythera, then with a look of regret on his face, Remus let go of Valentine's shoulders and stepped back. "Before you know it, you'll be back home, and we can have a late supper. I'll have your favorite food brought in."

Tears glittered in Valentine's eyes. "I only want you to do one thing for me."

"Anything, my dearest friend. Name it and it's yours."

"Make sure the Blood Moon Festival goes ahead. People can still celebrate tonight. I want you to remember me when you have fun."

"That's not advisable," Cythera said. "Besides, who'd want to celebrate after a murder has been committed on these grounds?"

"All the people refusing to take their tents down," I said. "There's a thirst for the festival, despite what's happened."

"Some people have no morals." Cythera glared at Remus. "Will you let us leave, or do I need to call in reinforcements?"

"Let her take me," Valentine said. "It's for the best."

After a few seconds of hesitation, Remus stepped aside.

Cythera tutted as she led Valentine away.

"Don't worry. We'll make sure he's treated fairly," Zandra said to Remus.

His shoulders sagged, and he looked at the floor. "He's my most loyal vampire, but he sometimes does foolish things because he thinks it's for the good of the hive. Please, make sure Cythera isn't hard on him. He's a fragile creature. He has a big heart."

"Of course. We'll look after him. Be back in a minute." I hurried after Cythera and Valentine as they walked to the back door and around the side of the house.

Cythera was speaking quietly to Valentine. He nodded in response and skulked beside her like a scolded hellhound pup.

"Before you go, there's something I'd like you to see." I hurried to catch up with Cythera.

She glanced back at me. "Does it have to do with Briar's murder?"

"No. But it's important. New graffiti has appeared on Remus's land. I believe it's connected to marks that have shown up around Crimson Cove."

"Why should I care about that?"

"Because you had angels on the case not so long ago," I said. "Whoever is doing this is spreading their net wider."

Cythera stopped and turned to me, one hand remaining on Valentine's elbow. "I can't think about a few graffiti daubs. I've just solved a murder. That's my priority."

"But they're—"

"No! Keeping a dangerous vampire off our streets is my focus." She turned and ushered Valentine along.

I trotted beside her, not ready to admit defeat with this prickly angel. "You'll investigate the daubings, though? I've been researching them, and—"

"And you're causing me trouble I don't need. Can't you see I'm busy enough as it is?"

I despised it when someone talked over me. "Not so long ago, that's all you cared about."

She sighed. "Things change. Don't you have mice to chase?"

"Not while you're questioning an innocent vampire about murder."

Valentine worried his bottom lip with his teeth. "It'll be okay. Everything will work out."

"Not for you," I said.

"For Remus. For the hive."

"Stop talking to this creature," Cythera snapped at him. "She loves to meddle where she's not wanted."

"I'm wanted!" I extended a paw. "We can continue our conversation if you let me hitch a ride to the station."

"Not happening. Ready?" Cythera said to Valentine.

Valentine gritted his teeth as she clamped her arms around him and shot into the air, leaving behind a waft of cool air and a few feathers that danced in the breeze.

I looked up the hill to where I'd seen the symbols. I'd hoped to get the angels on side to continue the investigation into those marks, but I'd picked the wrong angel and the wrong time to gain a willing recruit.

"Hey! Why chase after Cythera? You know where she's going." Zandra caught up with me.

"While she was here, I needed to tell her about those symbols."

Zandra furrowed her brow. "You think they're linked to Briar's murder?"

"No." I glanced at my wonderful witch. She needed to know more about these symbols, especially if trouble was coming our way. "They're linked to gremlins."

"Gremlins! We don't get many gremlins around here. I figured they were gang tags or people just messing around. You think they're something to worry about?"

"I do. I've been researching them. Those symbols need to go on our to-do list to figure out."

"Sure. If you think they're important. But first, the murder?"

"But first, the murder."

Zandra translocated us to Angel Force, so we were only a couple of minutes behind Cythera. But she'd been efficient and had already settled Valentine in an interview room and was barking orders to get the paperwork processed. Bertoli was in the room with Valentine, waiting for Cythera.

This time, we weren't allowed to join them, and had to sit next door and watch through the one-way mirror.

"Do you think she's punishing us?" Zandra muttered as she sank onto a plastic chair.

"Of course. Cythera is worried we'll solve the crime faster than her, like we usually do." I settled on my witch's lap. It had been a busy morning, and I needed a cat nap. I felt my eyes grow heavy as I gently made biscuits on her knees, being careful not to sink my claws through her jeans and make her squeak.

Cythera got Valentine's details, then began her questioning. "Tell me about your relationship with Briar Vixen."

Valentine kept his gaze down as he lifted one shoulder. "She was a food source. There's nothing else to tell you."

"Why did you pick her to feast on?"

"She was an easy target?"

"Is that a question you're asking yourself, or did you deliberately go after Briar?"

"Briar was pretty, and she smelled good. I have no more reasons to give you." Valentine raised his head an inch. "I killed her. Charge me and lock me up."

"Can you remember what Briar wore the night she died?" Bertoli said.

Valentine froze for a second. "Not really."

"A dress? T-shirt? Jeans?"

"Um... maybe a dress. I wasn't focused on her clothing."

"You like your designer clothes, though. Those jeans aren't cheap."

I blinked. Bertoli was being astute. His time away from Crimson Cove had honed his detecting skills and refined his tolerance for me and my witch.

"Did you have to remove any of her clothing to bite her?" Bertoli asked.

Valentine nibbled on his lower lip again. "No?"

"Another question? You're unsure?" Cythera inspected the paperwork she'd brought in with her.

"I was hungry and in a hurry."

"Were you working under anyone's orders?" she asked.

"No! Definitely not Remus's instructions. He had nothing to do with this."

"Of course, he'd say that," I said. "Cythera better not take this confession at face value."

"You think Valentine is lying to her?" Zandra lightly rested a hand on my head and massaged between my ears.

"I suspect Valentine overheard part of the conversation Remus was having with Cythera and panicked. He couldn't bear the thought of his master being imprisoned, so he threw out this confession to take the heat off Remus."

"Sacrificing himself for his master," Zandra said. "Makes sense. All vampires are fiercely loyal to their maker."

"Talk us through what you did with Briar," Bertoli said.

I let out a gentle sigh, relieved they were digging for more information.

"There's not much to tell. I convinced her to go into the woods with me and then I fed from her."

"Did she struggle?"

"Not much."

Bertoli glanced at Cythera. "Did you have any problems while you fed?"

I leaned forward. "He's referring to the messy neck holes."

"No. Briar was easy to feast on," Valentine said.

"Were there other vampires with you?" Cythera asked. "Did you have help?"

"Just me. I acted alone. There was no one else there, and no one ordered me to do this."

"Valentine is stressing no one else was involved," Zandra said.

"To take the blame and save Remus," I murmured. "Maybe he saw something that has him worried. Perhaps another vampire leading Briar away?"

Zandra nodded, her focus on the interview.

We listened some more while Cythera kept asking the same questions, and Valentine repeated the same vague answers.

"He didn't do this," I said. "Those clumsy marks on Briar's neck suggest a new vampire killed Briar."

"And Valentine can't even confirm what Briar wore," Zandra said. "Although guys can be like that. They're more interested in what's under the clothes."

"Not all guys are like that. I know a wonderful tech mage who'd adore you if you wore a cloth sack."

Zandra grunted. "Let's focus on the murder, and not on my lack of love life."

"I'm just saying, you don't need to label all men with the same letchy leerer brush."

"Fine. Most men are letchy leerers, not all."

After a few more moments of getting nowhere with Valentine, Cythera shoved back her seat and stood. "You're staying in the cells. We'll have more questions for you."

"You're not charging me? Don't you want my signed confession? I'm happy to give it to you." Valentine clutched the edge of the table separating him from the angels.

"Not yet. We have things to investigate before we bring formal charges against you."

Bertoli led a miserable Valentine away toward the cells.

The door to our room opened, and Cythera stood there, not looking happy. "You heard all the interview?"

"Of course. And you can't charge him based on that information," I said.

"Why not? He's confessed. It could hold up under scrutiny."

"You know it wouldn't. Valentine's answers were too vague. And they were vague because he didn't kill Briar."

Cythera pinched the bridge of her nose. "I agree. Valentine is covering for Remus. He's the vampire who should be behind bars."

I hopped off Zandra's comfy lap with some reluctance. "We should keep looking for better suspects."

Cythera stared down at me. "You really don't think Remus killed Briar?"

Zandra pushed herself out of the seat. "Remus can be slippery, but in the time I've known him, he's never come across as a dangerous vampire. He'd rather charm someone into submission than chew on them."

Cythera pushed a strand of blonde hair off her face. "It's not uncommon for vampires to slip. They all have that primitive seed that can flourish in the wrong conditions."

"Remus is a good vampire," I said. "However, there are a couple of young bucks who were vying for the victim's attention. Why don't we chat with them?"

Cythera stiffened. "I'm in charge around here. I decide who we question next."

I wriggled my booping snooter. "Then who should we talk to?"

She slumped forward. "Briar's boyfriend does seem an obvious target."

"And any of the gentlemen she made friends with at the festival?"

Cythera gritted her teeth. "Them, too."

"Excellent suggestion. Will you make the arrangements, or shall I?"

Chapter 11

Young bucks

After a break, which involved a nap, food, and a tickle from Zandra, we found ourselves on the right side of the law when Cythera invited us into the interview with Keanu Sweeny, the guy who'd been seen fighting over Briar with her boyfriend.

While we waited for Keanu to be brought into the interview room, I turned to Cythera. "I thought we were interviewing Briar's boyfriend first?"

"That was the plan, but we couldn't find Trent at the campsite. We asked around, and then spotted Keanu, so brought him in instead. He was next on the list, anyway."

"You don't think Trent has already left the area?" Zandra said.

"If he has, we'll bring him back. But I doubt he's left. He'll know better than to sneak off while an investigation into his girlfriend's murder takes place."

"Perhaps he's hiding for a reason," I said.

Cythera didn't look up from the paperwork she scanned. "If he is, we'll find him. I have everything under control."

"As always. We can rely on you," I said.

She snorted as she scribbled notes on a piece of paper.

A moment later, Keanu was brought in and settled in a seat by Bertoli, who then left the room. He was in his early thirties. New age guy attractive, with messy dark hair, corded multi-colored bangles around one wrist, and he wore tight jeans that looked uncomfortable to sit down in.

Cythera made the introductions, got Keanu to state his name and details, and then began the interview.

"Could you tell me about your relationship to Briar Vixen?"

"There's not much to tell. I barely knew her. I mean, we got to know each other at the festival, but that's it." He inspected his nails. "She was hot, flirty, and obviously interested in me, so we made out."

"You had an intimate relationship with her?" Cythera asked.

"Not really. She was cute and tipsy, so I figured, why not have fun?" Keanu leaned forward in his seat. "I heard a vampire got charged with killing her. Do you know why I broke up with my vampire girlfriend?"

Cythera hesitated, looked at her notes, and frowned. "You had a vampire girlfriend?"

"Because she sucked the life out of me." Keanu snorted a laugh. "Sorry, I joke under pressure."

"Why do you feel under pressure?" I asked.

His laughter faded. "I... I don't. I've got nothing to hide. I figured you'd brought me here to learn if I saw anything dodgy. You know, some crusty vamp dragging Briar to the woods to play hide the fangs."

"That's part of the reason," Cythera said. "Did you see Briar with a vampire the night she died?"

Keanu shook his head. "It's gotta be one, though, right? Everyone was talking about what happened to her. I went to the woods when everyone else was there, but it was too crowded, so I didn't see her body. But I heard she got bit. Two holes in the side of her neck. Classic vamp attack. Case solved."

"Apparently not, since we're still questioning suspects," Zandra said.

Keanu waved a hand in the air. "The angels need to show they're earning that money they get paid. Lock up the first vamp they capture and charge him, and it would look lazy. You gotta hunt around, prod some innocent folk, make them sweat. Am I right?"

"No, you're not," Cythera snapped.

"What magic do you have?" I asked Keanu. "Can you shapeshift?"

"Nothing so primitive. I'm a mishmash. My dad was a water wizard. Not sure what my mother was. She's long gone. Maybe she had no magic, since I've got nothing amazing." Keanu waggled his eyebrows. "I'm not the fanged beast you're looking for."

"Did you know Briar came to the festival with a boyfriend?" Cythera said.

"She may have come here with one, but they were fighting all the time. I figured she'd ditched him when she came on to me. Or not. I didn't care either way."

"Briar approached you?" Zandra said.

"Who could resist this?" Keanu grinned at her and winked. "And I was hardly going to say no. She was a pretty, flirty girl. She was flirting with everyone, though, so it got annoying. She flirted with the beer guy, the sandwich seller, and the brownie witch. It got boring."

More likely, Keanu got jealous because he couldn't hold Briar's attention. "You didn't like that?"

"Briar was fun, but she had no focus. All that fluttering around other guys. It's no surprise she got herself in a mess."

My hackles rose. "You think because she was flirting and spending time with other people, she deserved what happened to her?"

"No! I mean, I guess it didn't help. She was putting it out there, so she was a target. A lot of people noticed her. Briar stood out. She was a star, and she knew it."

The more this guy talked, the less I liked him. "What if I told you we're uncertain it was a vampire attack? Would you be surprised?"

Cythera shifted in her seat, but didn't tell me off for revealing our doubts about the killer.

"Yeah! Sure. I'd be shocked. But then I've only heard rumors about what happened. I didn't see anything." Keanu rocked his seat back. "It wasn't a vampire that bit her?"

"If it wasn't, can you think of anyone who wanted her dead?" Zandra picked up the line of questioning.

Keanu made a show of thinking, but it was a poor act. "Her crazy ex. Trevor? Trenton? Toby? I don't know. Some dumb name beginning with T. Those two kept snapping at each other. He was super possessive and never left her side for more than a few seconds. When she sent him off to get her food or drink, he'd watch her. It was creepy."

"It sounds like you spent a lot of time with Briar to have seen so much," I said.

Keanu's cheeks flushed. "No. I mean, she found me. She came on to me. We made out for like ten minutes, and then she rushed off to talk to someone. That was it."

"Yet you were aware of what her super possessive boyfriend was doing all evening," I said. "How would you know that if you weren't interested in Briar? Maybe even tracking her movements?"

Keanu shrugged. "I may have paid her attention. But she was cute and dressed to impress. And I'm just a guy. There's no harm in watching a pretty girl dance around." He shifted in his seat and crossed his arms over his chest. "Some days, I feel like it's a crime to be a man. You have to watch what you say to make sure you're not offending anyone."

"You have a hard life," I said.

He glared at me.

"Let's go through your movements for the evening of Briar's murder," Cythera said.

Keanu jerked upright in his seat. "My movements? Why do you care about them? I've told you everything I know. Briar was basically a stranger to me."

"Yet as my... consultant pointed out, you know a considerable amount about her movements. That suggests one of two things to me. Either you were more interested in Briar than you've revealed and were following her around the festival."

"No! Not that. What's the second option?"

"You're a super observer."

"Huh? What's that?"

"We have them in Angel Force. They're individuals with photographic memories. Once they see a face, they never forget it. It's an important skill to have when we're working on complicated criminal cases."

"Oh! I'm one of them. Yeah. I see a pretty face, and I never forget it. I'm a super observer." Keanu relaxed into his seat.

Cythera made a note on her paper. "That's highly unlikely."

I twitched my whiskers. Cythera was being sassy. I liked this side of her.

"So, your movements. Let's say you had an interest in Briar, and watched her as she went around the festival," Cythera said.

"I never said that. You said I did that. I told you, I'm just good with faces."

"Or you were stalking Briar?" I said.

Keanu rubbed his palms together several times. He sighed. "Not stalking. Maybe I was interested in Briar the second I saw her, so I stayed close by, waiting for a chance to talk to her. Like I said, her boyfriend stayed by her side, but I could tell she didn't like it. She kept sending him off. And

I overheard her complain to her sisters that she didn't realize he was so clingy."

"It must have annoyed you that Trent stopped you from getting access to Briar," I said.

"Nah. It was only a matter of time before I struck lucky with her." Keanu spread his arms wide, revealing broad shoulders and toned biceps. "I'm a catch. Women throw themselves at me. Briar was the same. I knew, when she got to know me, we'd have fun. We just needed to shake her boyfriend off our tail."

"Let's go back a step," Cythera said. "When did you first stalk Briar?"

"Not stalk!" Keanu rubbed the back of his neck. "I was at the café with the protestors. I'm not one of them. I don't cause trouble, but I pretended I was interested so I could tag along. These festivals always attract hot girls who like the grungy types. You know, the unwashed do-gooders who fake wanting to save the world and preach free love. Free handouts more like."

"You're drifting from the point," Cythera said. "Briar?"

"Sure. They just get me angry. I work hard while they hang out in fields and do nothing." Keanu raked a hand through his hair. "Anyway, I knew it wouldn't be long before I lucked out and bagged a hottie."

"So, you found your target and planned on creeping on Briar at the first opportunity?" I asked.

He held up his hands. "Hey! I'm not the monster here. I didn't creep on anyone. I'm a good looking, single guy who enjoys himself with the hot single girls looking for action."

Even Cythera smirked at his egotistical description.

"Go on," she said. "You saw Briar at the café, then you went to the festival? Alone or with her?"

"Alone. I kept my distance while she was with her boyfriend. But it didn't take me long to see they were unhappy. They argued about something, and he stormed off."

"That was when you made your move?" I asked.

"If you can call it a move. Briar was standing on her own. I could tell she was angry, so I caught her eye, and she smiled at me. She walked over and asked if I could keep her company. She said she'd had a fight with her boyfriend and didn't want to be alone."

"And, of course, you were happy to oblige," I said.

"Sure. We talked for a few minutes and then she laid a kiss on me. I barely had to do any work. It's usually what happens when you look like this. The ladies can't keep their hands to themselves."

"There have been reports you were seen fighting over Briar." Cythera consulted her notes. "Expand on that for me."

Keanu cracked his neck and rolled his shoulders. "It was nothing."

"You were fighting with Trent?"

"Kinda. Like I said, it wasn't important."

"What was the fight about?" Cythera said.

Keanu sighed. "Briar, of course. When that jerk realized he'd been replaced, he wasn't happy. He confronted her and tried to lay claim. I wouldn't back down when he told me to take a hike."

"How bad did the fight get?"

"Hurling insults. Nothing physical. I won't bruise these good looks for any woman, no matter how small her shorts are."

"Chivalrous to the end," I said.

"Yeah, whatever. Anyway, we argued for a while, then Briar told us we weren't good enough for her and stomped off. I think she was mad because I wouldn't thump Trent."

"Did you follow her?" Zandra asked.

"I was done with her. She wasn't even that great of a kisser. Too much teeth. I hate it when a girl bites you and gets dominant. You lay back and leave that to me, sweetheart. I'm the man around here."

"You seem cut up about your loss," I said.

"Err... not really. I'm not gonna fake being sad. I mean, it's not good news, someone getting it in the neck from a vamp, but it had nothing to do with me." Keanu leaned back. "We met, had fun, and moved on. End of story. I didn't see Briar after our make-out session."

"What did you do after Briar walked off?" Cythera said.

"Had a drink to cool down, then joined the next color dash. You know, the dry paint throwing thing. That took my mind off the drama and gave me a chance to find my next conquest. Some of those ladies had no shame. They were flinging their bras off and dancing almost naked. I got quite an eyeful. It almost made me blush." Keanu chuckled, a wistful look in his eyes.

This guy was a piece of work. I flexed my murder mittens, trying to think of a reason I could legitimately scratch him and not get thrown out by

Cythera. It would almost be worth it just to draw blood and make this creep pay.

Keanu seemed oblivious to my murder mitten restraint and jawed on about what a catch he was and how all the ladies wanted him. They most likely wanted him stuffed in a box and sent to a dark spot at the bottom of the ocean.

He jerked forward in his seat. "Hey! If you don't think a vampire did this to Briar, I know who you should speak to."

"Who would that be?" Cythera said.

"Sad sack Trent, or whatever his name is. The last time I saw him, he was buying a load of drinks from a stall. Then he went to his tent and was packing his kit. I reckon he's making a run for it. You know, escaping before the net closes in. I don't trust the guy. His eyes are too close together. Makes him look shifty."

"He was still at the festival camping site?" I was already shuffling toward Zandra, ready to spring into action.

"Yeah. His tent was near the back of the site. I was tempted to go over and offer my condolences. After all, we shared the same girl for a short time, so I know how he's feeling."

Cythera openly sneered at Keanu. "Of course you do."

He grinned at her, oblivious to the sarcasm. "If I was in charge of this case, that's who I'd track down, not the innocent hot guy who got messed up with a bad girl."

I hopped onto Zandra's shoulder. "If you'll excuse us. We have somewhere to be."

Chapter 12

Suspects afoot

"Translocation spell?" I whispered in Zandra's ear as we left the interview room.

"It's the quickest way to Oak Park Ridge. We need to make sure Trent isn't making a run for it."

The door to the interview room opened. Cythera stepped out and closed the door behind her. "Take Bertoli with you to the festival. I'll finish processing Keanu and then release him."

"You don't consider him a suspect anymore?" I paused in my creation of the translocation magic that would whisk us to Remus's mansion so we could catch our next suspect.

"We need to determine if he took part in the color dash, but if witnesses saw him, we must discount him."

"He's still shady," Zandra said. "He was lurking close to Briar, waiting to make his move."

"I agree. Keanu saw too much for it to be a coincidence," I said. "And with the chaos of the paint throwing, he could have dragged Briar away.

Maybe he wanted more from her, and she refused him."

"Or Briar was using him to get back at Trent, and Keanu found out," Zandra said.

"All things I'll take into consideration," Cythera said. "Find Trent. We need to know why he's so keen on leaving while his girlfriend's murder has yet to be solved. We have a photo ID of him. Bertoli will make copies so you can show it around."

After we got our picture of Trent to help locate him, we hurried out of the building. I cast a translocation spell, and we arrived outside Remus's mansion. Despite it being late in the afternoon, there were plenty of hungover looking people wandering around. There was also music playing and the smell of cooking meat in the air.

"The partying is still going on." Zandra strode toward a busy stallholder, who was giving out soft drinks.

"It's what Valentine wanted," I said. "Remus will respect his wishes and keep the fun going."

"What will it be?" the guy giving out drinks said as we reached the counter.

"We're looking for this guy. Trent Masters." Zandra held out the picture we'd grabbed from Bertoli.

"He looks like a lot of the trendy types around here."

"Trent may have bought supplies from you before he left. Take a good look."

The seller scratched his chin. "Maybe I saw him. It's hard to say. These guys all look the same to me."

Zandra turned, and we took a moment to survey the crowd. He was right. There were several guys with black painted fingernails and guyliner smeared under their eyes, posing in tight jeans and groovy band T-shirts.

"I'll let you know if I see him," the guy said. "Sure you don't want anything?" His gaze shifted behind us to a growing queue.

"No. Thanks." Zandra stepped away.

"There's Bertoli!" I said. He'd arrived in a bluster of wings, making the crowd part as he landed.

Zandra hurried over to him. "We figured we'd start with the food and drink stalls. Keanu said he saw Trent getting supplies."

"Works for me. I'll check the campsite and ask around." Bertoli hurried off.

We spent the next half an hour searching for Trent, but kept getting the same response. No one remembered him, and they rightly pointed out a large percentage of festivalgoers looked like him, so he'd be hard to pick out from the crowd. And as the music got louder, and the sun sank, it became harder to get people's attention. They were more interested in partying than answering questions about murder suspects.

"That's one of Remus's vampires." I gestured at a tall, well-built guy with a crew cut, wearing a red velvet tuxedo jacket with a large white rose in the lapel. "Let's find out what the plans are for the festival."

Zandra strode over to him. "Hey, it's Henry, isn't it?"

He turned and nodded. "Henri, actually. My mother was French, if you want to say it with a fancy accent, but Henry is close enough. Are you and Juno joining in the fun tonight?"

"We're still looking for Briar's killer. Remus is definitely keeping the event going?" I asked.

"Of course. He's calling it the post-Blood Moon celebration. We wanted to do something special for Valentine. Remus refuses to let Angel Force spoil the fun. Valentine loves a party, and we wanted him to know we're thinking of him and the stupidly noble confession he made."

"You don't think he killed Briar?" Zandra asked.

"Not a chance. He's too loyal for his own good, though. I suppose we'd have all done the same to protect Remus if we thought he was about to be charged with murder. Valentine is known for getting the wrong end of the stick about things. It lands him in trouble." Henri pursed his lips. "He loves Remus. We all do. This hive is our world, and we'll do anything to protect it. Valentine will be home soon. I should get on and make sure the fun is ready."

Zandra walked along beside Henri as he walked away. "What fun are you planning?"

"I found a ton of fireworks in the basement and figured we'd let them off all at once, so Valentine will hear them and know they're for him." Henri gestured at the crowd. "We're going out with a bang."

"Good to know. Have you seen this guy?" Zandra held out the picture of Trent.

Henri stared at it for a few seconds, then shook his head. "I don't know him. He's not from around here, but that's all I can tell you."

"It's important we find him. He's wanted in connection to the murder."

His eyes widened. "Why didn't you say? I can get some help to look for him. Most of the vampires are awake now the sun is going down. You think he killed Briar?"

"We're not certain. But we heard he was packing his things and leaving. Trent used to date Briar," I said.

"Sound suspicious. We can't let him leave. Not with Valentine in the frame and the angels still grumbling about shutting the party." Henri stuck his fingers in his mouth and whistled, then grinned at us. "Remus hates it when I do that, but it gets everyone's attention. We'll roust this guy and teach him a lesson. No unpermitted killing on Remus's land. Is Trent a vampire? Have we got a rogue in our midst?"

"Not so fast," Zandra said. "We don't even know he's guilty. We just need to talk to him."

"A little gentle rousting isn't a bad idea," I said.

"You'll be suggesting we obliterate him next," Zandra muttered.

"We can move much faster than you," Henri said. "We'll stop this guy from sneaking away."

"Trent may not be sneaking anywhere." Zandra tucked the picture into her jacket pocket. "Our source wasn't that reliable."

"True. Keanu may have been deflecting attention by pointing the finger of blame elsewhere," I said. "And the bitter boyfriend is an obvious target."

"What does he smell like?" Henri said.

"Can't help you there," Zandra said. "I don't sniff everyone I meet."

Henri smirked. "Juno? Did you get a good sniff of Trent at any point?"

"Sadly not."

"I'll get everyone looking. I'll let you know when we have him." Henri bounced on his toes, excited by the prospect of hunting Trent. I almost felt sorry for the guy, but not if he was trying to get away with murder.

By this time, several more vampires had arrived. Henri showed them Trent's picture and then they raced away, their movement so fast, their forms blurred before my eyes.

"I'm not sure it was such a great idea to get the vampires hunting Trent," Zandra said. "We don't want them getting over-excited."

"They're motivated and speedy. Cythera isn't here to help us look, and since we haven't heard from Bertoli, he must have gotten lost among the tents."

"Or he found Trent and took him in without telling us." Zandra twisted her mouth to the side.

"Bertoli would never do that. He's a reformed angel with deliciously pink wings. We're friends."

Zandra snorted a laugh. "If you say so. Let's keep watch and make sure the vampires don't get too frenzied on their hunt."

"We can do that while finishing questioning stallholders. I noticed a bratwurst stand that smells divine. We haven't been there yet."

Zandra rolled her eyes, but didn't protest as I led her toward sausage heaven.

We carried on along the row of food stalls, asking if anyone had seen Trent. I got a smoky, drool-worthy German sausage, and then we stopped at Edith Emory's Enchanting Eats and showed her Trent's picture.

She nodded as she offered free samples. "I know that, young man."

I swallowed my last bite of sausage. "Have you seen Trent recently?"

"Not today. But he got into an argument over the poor girl who was killed."

"We know he was fighting with another guy over Briar," I said.

"And Trent had a right to defend her. I always watch for the men who creep after young ladies when their guard is down. It happens at almost every event. I can't stand it."

"That's what you think happened to Briar?" I said.

"I'm sorry to say it's possible. And there was one guy who kept following her around. He was intense. I didn't like him."

"Can you describe him to us?" Zandra said.

Edith set down a brownie box and wrinkled her brow. "Early thirties. New age looking with dark hair that needed a comb. He had multi-colored bangles on one wrist. Oh! And his jeans! They were so tight they left nothing to the imagination." Her cheeks flushed.

"That sounds like Keanu. He was stalking Briar," I murmured to Zandra.

Edith nodded. "He kept his distance, but he was always staring at her. When she argued with that young man in the picture, the creeper was by her side a couple of minutes later."

"The creepy guy, Keanu, approached Briar after she fought with Trent?" I said.

"He did. I watched his every move. I didn't trust him."

"How did Briar respond?"

"She didn't object to his company. She was tense at first, but then relaxed and started laughing. I watched them for several minutes to make sure his interest wasn't unwelcome. I'd have said something if it was. I won't have the ladies bothered. If he'd become a problem, I'd have whacked him with a brownie tray and sent him on his way."

"How long would you say Keanu was watching Briar?" I asked.

"I can't be certain because I was busy that evening, but I saw him following her on three occasions. That young woman had boundless energy and couldn't keep still. She kept dragging her sisters with her, too. Every time she passed my stand, a few seconds later, the same guy followed her. Keanu, did you say?"

I nodded. "And Trent saw what was going on?"

"He must have done. Briar argued with him, and then he left. That's when Keanu slid over. Then her boyfriend returned, and they fought. It was very tense."

"What was the outcome of the fight?"

"People pulled them apart. It didn't get that physical, mainly shouting and a few pushes. I'm not sure either of them wanted a fistfight."

"What was Briar doing when they were arguing over her?" Zandra asked.

"Watching. I was some distance away, but she seemed to enjoy them fighting over her. I suppose it's an ego thing, isn't it? A beautiful young woman being fought over by two eligible bachelors." Edith patted her hair. "Men used to fight over me when I was in my prime."

"I'd never describe Keanu as eligible," I muttered in Zandra's ear.

"How did the fight end?" Zandra said.

"The men separated and were encouraged to walk away. Briar had walked off by then, too."

"Did they leave each other alone?"

"Yes. I even called Keanu over to give him advice on picking the right lady friend. I didn't want anyone hurt because his blood was up."

"How did he take that advice?" I asked.

Edith bustled about the stand. "Not well. He was rude to me. I won't repeat what he said, but it was something about my age and sticking things where the sun doesn't shine. I had to sit down and eat a brownie to recover. One of my calming blends. Would you like one?" She pointed to a tray of macadamia topped caramel brownies.

"No. But thanks. That's useful information," I said. "And you're sure you haven't seen Trent today?"

"I haven't served him, but he may have wandered past and I missed him. Is it important you see him?"

"We have questions about the investigation into what happened to Briar," I said.

"Oh! Well, I hope you find him. I haven't heard anyone's been charged yet. Have they?" Edith raised her eyebrows. "People keep talking about it when I serve them."

"The angels are still investigating," Zandra said. "Thanks again."

We hurried away from the stand.

"So, Keanu was stalking Briar. He lied to us," I said. "What else has he lied about? Maybe his alibi?"

"We should tell Cythera not to let him go. If she does, he might be the one who makes a run for it."

Henri raced over, his cheeks glowing. "I've got news about your missing guy. He left twenty minutes ago. Someone saw him packing a bag and then he vanished. He even left his tent behind."

"Why the hurry?" Zandra said. "You think he'd stick around to find out what happened to his girlfriend."

"Unless he already knows the answer," I said. "We can still find him. Trent will only know the major routes in and out of town."

"We'll block the roads," Henri said.

"You can't do that. You don't have the right permissions in place." Bertoli strode over.

"We must catch Trent," I said. "Henri has offered his services to track him."

Bertoli's wings fluttered, then he nodded. "That's appreciated. But we can't block the roads. It would cause too much chaos, and we need to get authorization."

"You're gonna let some dumb paperwork stop you from catching a killer?" Henri flexed his hands.

"We can post watches on the main routes in and out," I said. "Grab Trent before he gets too far."

"We should split up," Zandra said. "Each take a road. If we're quick, we'll stop him from leaving."

"What do you say, Bertoli? Want to be the hero of the hour?" I said.

He scrubbed at a pink tinged wing. "Let's do it."

After a speedy allocation of routes between Bertoli, the assisting vampires, Zandra, and me, we went our separate ways.

I was rushing along a path that led to the road when I slowed. Fresh symbols had been left on the wall in plain sight, alongside a set of painty paw prints. And those paw prints led off through the trees. These symbols had only just been created.

With a paw raised, I hesitated. I had to know who was leaving them and what mischief they had planned. If I was quick, I could catch them.

The prints grew fainter as whoever had made them hurried away, but I was able to pick up a few white spots here and there. There was a familiarity to the scent they left behind, too. I should know that smell, but it was mingled with something that made my toe beans tingle uncomfortably.

I rounded a corner, and my breath whooshed out of me when I saw Sammy.

Chapter 13

Snuggle buddy returns

I blinked several times, my heart spasming. Sammy was back! Was he the one making those symbols?

I hurried along behind him. His step was brisk, but he was slunk low to the ground, scuttling away like a startled crab. He looked thin, and there was a worrying haze of gray magic around him.

Sammy's magic had never been gray. But the last time I'd touched him, I'd sensed an unsettling flavor to his power. I'd assumed his magic had been wounded when he was mistreated by the demon. But that demon was locked away and shouldn't have any influence over Sammy. But something bad had grabbed him by the throat and was forcing him to leave these damaging symbols everywhere.

Why would Sammy want to harm Crimson Cove with gremlin chaos? Did he even know what trouble those symbols could conjure?

I kept him in my sights as we journeyed through the trees. Should I take him down and confront him? I had more of my magic in place than the last time I'd challenged him, but I'd barely used it since my tail disappeared for fear of it backfiring. What if I used a spell on Sammy and it injured him?

Despite all the damage he'd done to Crimson Cove and our relationship, I was glad to see him. There'd been a time when I worried he'd perished from his injuries.

I was conflicted. Treat Sammy like the enemy, or a dear friend who desperately needed help?

Sammy broke into a run, and I increased my pace and dashed after him. He kept going, his ears back and his tail down. What had got my guy so spooked?

I stumbled when he glanced over his shoulder and looked at me. He knew I was following him? Had he known the whole time? Did Sammy want me to follow him?

"Sammy! Wait. I want to talk. I need to know you're okay."

He turned in a half circle, heading back to the campsite.

I veered off the path and through the trees, hoping to cut him off, but he was too fast and had already sped along the path, and was almost out of sight.

"Sammy, what's going on?" My heart almost beat out of my chest as I blasted along the path, desperate to catch him.

He continued back toward the festival. Maybe he hoped to hide in the crowd and lose me.

I continued my frantic pursuit of my former snuggle bunny, my chest tight and my paws hurting. I wouldn't lose him. Not this time. I was getting Sammy back.

I reached the edge of the trees and slowed to a trot, scanning the grounds. There he was! Heading toward a crowd of partygoers dancing around a small bonfire. Sammy grew closer to the crowd, and the cloud of gray magic around him expanded, causing them to scatter and cringe away.

Sammy was heading toward the tents. He slowed, his head lifting as he looked around. That gave me a chance to gain on him, but there was still too much distance between us.

I conjured a knockdown spell. Since Sammy was ignoring me, I'd have to do this the hard way and trust my magic wouldn't let me down. I needed answers, and I had to know what he was doing.

I was about to throw the spell when Sammy plunged through the opening of a large green tent with tiny flags fluttering around the opening.

He was trapped! There was only one way out of that tent. As I reached the entrance, there was a shriek from inside and Trent Masters tumbled out. He lay on the grass panting and clawing at his face.

"Trent?" I raced over, my focus on the tent, waiting for Sammy to leap out and attack both of us.

Trent glanced at me, shaking his head, then looking down at his body and brushing his hands over his face repeatedly. "Do I know you?"

"Are you okay?" I couldn't see what had scared him. There was nothing unusual on his clothing or face that would make him wipe at his skin repeatedly.

"No. I'm... I'm not sure. Something weird just happened." Trent rolled onto his side and deep breathed for a few seconds, while inspecting the backs of his hands.

I stepped closer, still watching the tent. "Are you hurt?"

"No. Don't think so. I just... that was freaky." He kept brushing at his face.

"I work with Angel Force. We have to talk about Briar Vixen, but I need you to wait here for a minute. Go nowhere." I poked my head into the tent. Sammy was inside, staring at the canvas and stepping from paw to paw, anxiety bristling off him. "Sammy!"

He looked at me, hissed, blasted a hole through the side of the tent, and shot out of it.

"Don't go!" I backed out of the tent and discovered Trent had also made a run for it. I growled as I spotted him a few yards away, shoving people out of his path.

I looked at the hole in the tent and then at Trent. I wanted Sammy back, but we had a murder to solve. With a disgruntled snarl and fury heating my blood, I chased Trent. My knockdown spell was primed, so I slammed it into his back and sent him into the dirt before jumping on top of him and pinning him.

I looked over my shoulder, but there was no sign of Sammy. "Don't move," I growled out.

Trent squeaked. "What do you want with me? I've done nothing wrong."

"Your girlfriend's been murdered and you're making a run for it. That makes you guilty of something." I hissed in his ear. I was furious. Sammy had been within paw touching distance, and I'd had to let him go to deal with this idiot.

"That's got nothing to do with me. I just want to leave. I want no trouble."

"Trouble has found you. Move a muscle, and I'll bite you." I tugged on my bond with Zandra, letting her know I needed her assistance.

She appeared a few seconds later in a flash of magic, and her eyes widened. "You got him!"

"You don't know the sacrifice I had to make to do it. Trent was hiding in someone else's tent."

"Hiding, huh?" Zandra stood over him, her arms folded. "What have you got to hide from?"

Trent squirmed beneath my paws. "Get this creature off me! She's almost as bad as the other one."

"Other one?" Zandra glanced at me.

My unexpected encounter with Sammy had shaken me, and had to take several deep breaths before I could say his name. "Sammy is back."

Her mouth dropped open. "What! You sure? I thought he was... well, he's been gone so long."

"I'm certain. I chased him through the woods. I thought he was trying to get away, but he led me to Trent. He was helping me."

"Where is he?" Zandra looked around as a small crowd gathered to see what a witch and her awesome familiar were doing, pinning some loser to the ground.

"He left. He wouldn't talk to me. And there's something off with his magic. I didn't get close enough to touch him, but it feels rancid. It scared people when he got near them."

"Hey! I'm still down here," Trent said. "And I'm innocent of all crimes, so you can let me up."

"Highly doubtful," I said. "What did that other cat do to you?"

Trent twisted his head to the side as he attempted to look at me. "Your freaky attack cat, you mean?"

I growled. "The stunning tabby who cornered you in the tent. How did he know you were in there?"

"No clue. I've never seen him before. I figured you sent him in. Can I get up yet?"

"No," I said at the same time as Zandra. "What did Sammy do to you?"

"Err... not sure. I got hit with a gross feeling in the heart. It ran down me, and it felt like he was draining me of energy. I couldn't breathe and my head spun. I had to get out of there. And my skin was on fire."

"That doesn't sound like Sammy's magic," Zandra said.

"It was definitely him. I'd recognize Sammy in a crowd of tabby cats. He's unwell. I should have gone after him and not tackled this idiot." I glanced up to see sympathy in Zandra's eyes. "And... I think he's behind those symbols that have been appearing."

Her eyebrows rose. "Let's take Trent in. Then we'll figure out what to do about Sammy."

Trent struggled beneath my paws. "Take me in where? I want to leave."

"The only place you're going is an Angel Force interview room. They have questions for you," I said. "So, behave. Or I'll bring Sammy back and he'll teach you a lesson you'll never forget."

Trent shuddered. "Fine. I'll go with you. Just keep that monster away from me."

The fact Trent had called Sammy a monster left a lump of spiky pain in my gut. I hopped off Trent, and Zandra pulled him to his feet.

"You okay to round up the vampires and Bertoli? Let them know what's going on?" Zandra said to me.

I nodded. I was happy to have a distraction. My mind was a whirl of confusion and questions. Had Sammy helped with this investigation? Why were those people so afraid of him? Surely his magic couldn't be that polluted by the brief time he'd spent under the influence of a demon? And why was he putting those gremlin chaos symbols everywhere?

As I trotted away to find Bertoli and the vampires, the key questions on my mind were, what had happened to my wonderful Sammy? And how could I get him back?

Chapter 14

Secrets revealed

"He's not talking." Finn closed the door to the interview room and strode into the kitchen.

I followed him, Zandra beside me. "Which suggests he's hiding something."

"Could be." Finn made a coffee for him and Zandra and placed a bowl of water in front of me. "He's also demanding legal representation."

"Definitely shady if he's insisting on having a lawyer," Zandra said.

"There's a complication, though." Finn handed Zandra a mug. "Trent's mother is the lawyer he wants to represent him. And I recognize her name. She's a pit bull. When she gets her teeth into a case, she doesn't let go until she gets victory."

"And when she learns her son is being questioned about Briar's murder, she'll want to shake the angels until they let him go," I said.

"That's what I'm thinking," Finn said. "Bertoli is getting in touch with her. Until she gets here, Trent is saying nothing."

"We could try some mild threats on him," I said. "That could loosen his tongue before his mother arrives to spoil everything."

"Cythera did a fair amount of looming and wing fluttering, but he won't break. We're sticking him in a cell overnight and letting him stew. We'll pick up the interview in the morning." Finn rocked back on his heels and sighed.

Finn and Zandra drank coffee in silence while I lapped some water. This was a complication we could do without.

"If there's nothing more we can do to help, we'll get out of here," Zandra said. "Leave you to it. Let us know when you have news on Trent?"

"Will do. But I doubt we'll achieve anything tonight."

Zandra downed her coffee. "See you later."

We headed out of Angel Force.

I hopped onto Zandra's shoulder. "I know you probably need a break, but I must look for Sammy."

"I figured you'd say as much." She rested a hand on my side. "Let's grab something to eat, and then we can go searching."

I leaned my head against my wonderful witch. She was always there to support me.

Fifteen minutes later, and after grabbing a sandwich for Zandra and some jerky for me, we were on the road in the van and headed to the campsite to take another look at the symbols.

"Fill me in on these marks," Zandra said. "What have they got to do with Sammy being back in town?"

"Hopefully, nothing. But I've seen these symbols showing up around Crimson Cove. I first noticed them when we investigated Erig Morfiel's murder. They'd been placed near the graffiti that's been showing up."

"The graffiti we think Gaian and his gang are making?"

"Yes. And I'm yet to be convinced he isn't involved. Although I'm not sure if he's leaving the symbols, too. I wondered if the perpetrator used the graffiti tags to distract the eye, while leaving their nefarious symbols in a discreet location."

"For what purpose? What do they do?"

"I've seen them before, but I had to do research to refresh my memory. They belong to what I thought was an extinct gremlin cult. Chaos makers."

Zandra grimaced. "Gremlins love disorder. What do they want with Crimson Cove?"

"I'm uncertain. The symbols act as markers of intent. And their effect is cumulative."

"The more symbols, the more chaos?"

"Basically, yes."

"Have you seen any gremlins?" Zandra said.

"No. And this is where Sammy comes in. I saw him at a site of some freshly made symbols, and he had white paint on his paws."

"Sammy is hanging with the gremlins? Doing their bidding?"

"I don't know. I need to speak to him to see why he made them."

"Maybe he saw them and was curious. He touched the paint and got it on his paws," Zandra said. "I can't see Sammy getting in with a bunch of chaos making gremlins."

"Just like I didn't see Sammy as the kind of adorable creature who'd hang out with a demon, but we know how that story goes."

Zandra tickled my head. "We'll figure it out. If Sammy is out there, we'll get him back and make sure he's okay. I know you miss him."

I chewed on my final piece of jerky. I never thought I'd fall for someone like Sammy, but there'd been a piece of my heart missing since he'd left me.

Zandra pulled the van into an empty spot, and we climbed out. "Is there any reason the symbols are also showing up in Oak Park Ridge?"

"I'm concerned whoever is leaving them has up-scaled their plans. It was bad enough to think they were targeting Crimson Cove, but if they're spreading their chaos net wider, it'll be harder to contain."

We headed past the tents and several large groups of partygoers. The atmosphere seemed subdued, even though there was music playing and food stalls still serving. Maybe people had decided they weren't in the mood to party after all. And now the Blood Moon was on the wane, the magic in the air was palpably weaker.

We walked up the small hill and stopped by the stone where I'd seen the first set of symbols.

Zandra crouched and examined them. "Is there a pattern in these markings?"

"Yes, but it appears chaotic. It's done deliberately, so people see random splodges and dots. But my research revealed the pattern is significant.

And there needs to be a certain number of these symbols in an area before the chaos kicks off."

"And when it does?"

"We don't want to be around. The result won't be pretty."

She stood. "Are there more?"

"In the woods. That's where I saw Sammy."

We headed down the hill and along the trail. I found the markings, and we spent a few moments inspecting them.

Zandra tugged on her hair. "Why keep this from me?"

I curled around her legs. "At first, I didn't know what I was looking at. Besides, I didn't want to worry you."

"Juno! That's what I'm here for. We're a team. We take the good and the bad together."

"I know. I'm sorry. I wanted to figure things out before I got you involved. And you've been so busy at work..." my words trailed off.

"That's an excuse. I know you don't like involving me in dangerous situations, but that's what we do. We see problems and we fix them." She crouched and rested a hand on my head. "When we moved to Crimson Cove, I figured we'd only help animals in need, but the longer we're here, the more we seem to help people, too."

"Because you're a good witch with a strong sense of justice." I pressed my forehead against her thigh.

"And you're a good familiar. You just have a terrible habit of concealing important things from me." Her hand brushed across the stump where my magnificent tail once was.

"I'll do better." But some things needed to be kept from my wonderful witch. At least, for now.

We shared a moment of comfortable silence, Zandra gently stroking her fingers through my fur while I leaned against her.

This was the first time I'd ever experienced a true, pure, familiar bond. I'd had my share of disasters, bonding with powerful magic users who I hoped to exploit to get my power back. I never thought I'd find such a strong connection with one person. But here it was, and it was glorious.

"Shall we look around to see if there are any signs of Sammy?" Zandra said. "Maybe he has a base close by."

"That's what we're here for. And we'll look for more symbols, too."

We searched and searched until the moon was dipping in the sky. I was exhausted. Zandra was staggering on her feet, and we hadn't gotten so much as a glimpse of my wonderful tabby friend. Well, former friend.

I paused, one paw in the air. Something was approaching through the trees. A heavy-footed something. And it wasn't alone.

Zandra crouched beside me. "You hear that? Think it's a werewolf?"

"It doesn't smell like one. But whatever it is, it's heading for us." I drew in a breath and fluffed my fur, readying a freeze spell, just in case.

A gray blur blasted from a bush and slammed into me, taking me off my paws and rolling me across the dirt, twigs and stones jabbing me as I was tumbled. The sharp sting of teeth digging into my leg had me howling, and I slammed the freeze spell into my frenzied attacker.

Zandra threw out a dazzling spell, too, which covered me and my assailant, making my skin itch.

"Retreat!" a deep male voice rumbled. "Let go of the cat."

The teeth disappeared from my throbbing leg, and I rolled several more times before landing on my belly. I recognized that voice. It was Gaian.

I crouched, my gaze darting around, looking for my attacker. A gray, wiry hound stood by Gaian's leg, looking at me with hunger in its icy stare. It was joined by two more hounds, who watched me with hunger and the promise of death in their eyes.

Zandra scooped me up and inspected my leg. "You're bleeding!" She placed a hand over the wound and pulsed healing magic over me.

"My apologies if your familiar was injured," Gaian said. "The hounds were restless and needed a walk."

"Your hound tried to kill Juno!" Zandra stalked toward Gaian, magic fizzling on her fingertips. "If you can't control them, keep them on leashes and muzzle them, or they'll kill someone."

Gaian looked vaguely chastised. "Sorry, again. I didn't think anyone would be out so late." There was a question in his eyes.

"That's no excuse." Zandra stroked me, her movements rapid and shaky.

Gaian ran a hand through his hair. "The hounds see Juno as prey, since she's so small."

"I may be small, but I'm mighty. If your hounds come after me again, I'll obliterate them. That's your only warning. If you value them, keep them away from me." I wasn't happy there was a quiver in my voice.

Gaian looked momentarily startled before regaining his composure. "Understood. I'll keep them under control." He looked around the quiet wood. "Couldn't sleep?"

My leg felt better, so I scrambled out of Zandra's arms and onto her shoulder, glaring at the hounds. "We're investigating a mystery."

"You're involved in that murder investigation I've been hearing about?"

"That, too," I said.

"There's more mystery in Crimson Cove?" Gaian rubbed his chin. "As soon as Sorcha brought me here, I sensed this wasn't your average small town magic community."

"Crimson Cove attracts interesting characters." Since we'd stumbled into Gaian without Sorcha glued to his side, this was the perfect time to winkle out his dark secrets. "We've discovered disturbing symbols around the area. Would you know anything about them?"

"Disturbing symbols?" Gaian shook his head. "What are we talking about?"

Zandra's shoulders tensed, but I gently dug in my claws to let her know I had a handle on the situation.

I took a few seconds to orientate myself. "Zandra, take us to the location of the second markings. Let's show Gaian what is troubling us."

"What are you doing?" she muttered under her breath as she turned and headed along an overgrown path.

I shoved my booping snooter against her ear. "I want to see Gaian's reaction. If he's involved, he'll be surprised anyone has identified what those symbols mean."

Ten minutes later, we stood by the symbols in the wood and showed them to Gaian.

"They look like the work of an amateur," he said.

"They mean nothing to you?" I peered at his face, looking for a flicker of deceit, but his expression was impassive.

"I can't imagine they mean anything to anyone. If you like, I can get my guys to clean them off."

"Why would you do that?" Zandra said.

Gaian shrugged. "This place is growing on me, so I'm thinking of sticking around. And I've already talked to Sorcha about getting together a crew of volunteers to remove the graffiti. We can include these markings too, if you like."

"Won't you be too busy protesting about Remus's Blood Moon Festival?" I said.

"That's winding down. And after everything that happened on the first night, no one is in the mood to cause more trouble for the vampires. They're dealing with enough, since one of their own went rogue." Gaian smiled, but it didn't reach his eyes. "If we can lend a hand with your investigation, consider us willing helpers. I want to contribute positively to my new home. Everyone in the gang does."

"Thanks. We appreciate that," Zandra said cautiously.

"Sorry I can't figure out what these symbols mean. I'm sure they're nothing to worry about, though.

Enjoy the rest of your night." Gaian hesitated for a second, then strode away with his hideous hounds at his heel.

"He was surprisingly helpful," Zandra said.

"Too helpful. Maybe he was covering his tracks," I muttered. "I still don't trust him."

"Neither do I." She checked my leg again. "That's enough excitement. Let's go home."

I sighed. "We didn't find so much as a hint of Sammy."

Zandra hugged me. "We will. But not tonight."

Despite having been almost cross-eyed with tiredness when we finally got home, I hadn't slept, and a cloud of tired grumpiness hung over me as I headed to breakfast with Zandra the next morning.

I joined an equally grumpy Sage at the table, yawning a greeting as I settled into my seat.

"What's eating you?" she grumbled.

"I had a surprise yesterday. I saw Sammy."

Sage's head swiveled in my direction. "He's back in Crimson Cove?"

"I wasn't able to stop him and question him to learn if it was a flying visit or he'd come home for good. It was definitely him. I was out late last night with Zandra, looking for him."

"How did he seem?"

"Not himself. Troubled. And skinny. The skinny look doesn't suit him."

Sage huffed. "We've both been handed a dollop of bad luck. Ember still won't leave."

"Did you confront him?"

"I did. Vorana had to serve a customer with a cat allergy, so she left him behind the counter. He said we shook on the deal and I couldn't go back on it."

"I thought you were clear with Ember that it was just a trial?"

"I was! But he won't listen to sense. Hateful kitten." Sage grumbled for a few seconds. "Vorana is making him his own papoose, yet he walks fine. He doesn't need one. But he cries every time she puts him down. I've never encountered such a spiteful little runt."

As Sage groused about Ember encroaching on her territory, I kept silent. I wanted to share my concerns with her about Sammy, the symbols, and the murder investigation, but she was focused on her own problems, so I wouldn't burden her with more.

We'd settled in for breakfast, and Zandra was updating Vorana on the investigation, when she got a message on her mobile snow globe.

She pulled it out of her pocket and opened the message. "It's from Finn. They're setting up the interview with Trent. His mother has arrived, so he's willing to answer questions."

"Is he a murder suspect?" Vorana said. "I've barely seen you to ask how things are going?"

"He is. And things are going slowly." Zandra grabbed a banana muffin and gave me ten seconds to eat my smoked salmon before scooping me up. "Sorry, but we need to run."

"Of course! Go! But I want to hear everything later," Vorana said.

I glanced at her lap. Ember was fake sleeping, curled into a ball inside a fluffy papoose.

When I had a moment, I'd speak to that scallywag and tell him to stop stressing Sage. She was an elderly cat and deserved more respect.

But right now, we had a murder suspect to interrogate.

Chapter 15

Dead end to murder

The Angel Force office was busy when we arrived. There were half a dozen angels bustling around, getting their orders for the day, processing paperwork, and checking files.

Finn spotted us and gestured us to join him. "You're right on time. Trent's been consulting with his mother. He's willing to talk now he has her support."

"What's the mother like?" I asked.

"Kind of terrifying. Beautiful, but terrifying. You'll have to sit next door and watch the interview. Cythera wants this done by the book so the lawyer mother can't pull us apart and get the case thrown out on a technicality."

"A wonderful witch with advanced magic and a hyperintelligent cat with a fount of knowledge are hardly technicalities," I muttered.

Finn chuckled. "I know. You're awesome. But the boss is yet to see sense about you. We can't mess this up."

"Did Trent talk while he was here overnight?" Zandra asked.

"Not a peep. I get the impression it's not the first time he's been in trouble with the law. He knows how to work the system."

"And, most likely, his mother got him off of any misdemeanor he's caused, so he has no criminal record," I said. "This should be an interesting interview."

Five minutes later, we were settled in our regular seats, watching as Cythera and Finn ran through the formalities before starting the interview.

"Please describe your relationship to Briar Vixen," Cythera said.

Trent leaned over to his mother, who whispered in his ear. She was immaculately dressed in a tailored cream suit, her dark hair tied off her slim face in a ponytail.

"We dated," Trent finally said.

"For how long?"

"It was casual. We'd been together a couple of months. We weren't exclusive."

"But my client cared very much for the girl," his mother said, her voice an accent free tone of professionalism.

"You came to the festival with Briar and her sisters?" Cythera said.

Trent nodded. "Briar asked me to come with her."

"Did you encounter any problems at the festival?"

Trent leaned over and consulted quietly with his mother. "No problems."

"No disagreements with Briar?"

He licked his lips, but shook his head. "We got along fine."

Cythera consulted the file in front of her. "Then why do I have witness statements that show you argued with Briar on the evening of her murder?"

Trent gulped. "I... It was nothing. I forgot."

His mother tugged on his arm, and her whispering grew frantic.

"Trent's been keeping things from her," I said.

"He looks nervous," Zandra said. "Do you reckon he did it?"

"Trent's got a motive. Briar sounded like a flirt, not that there's anything wrong with that, but maybe she flirted one too many times and Trent snapped. He told her to behave, they fought, and things got vicious."

"If it was him, we come back to the problem of how he drained her?" Zandra leaned back in her seat.

"That's the sticking point to all of this." I nodded thoughtfully as I watched the interview.

"I'm sorry. I didn't mean to hide the argument," Trent said after his mother had whispered to him for several minutes. "I had nothing to do with what happened to Briar. The last time I saw her, she was alive."

"What was your argument about?" Cythera said.

"It was nothing serious. All couples argue."

"It was serious enough for you to storm away and leave her on her own."

"I didn't know anything bad would happen to her! And Briar wasn't on her own. She'd brought her sisters with her. They were always hanging around together."

"So, what did you argue about?" Cythera repeated.

Trent sighed. "Other guys kept hitting on her. It annoyed me, so I asked her to tone things down. Briar got mad. She told me I was a jealous loser. It got out of hand, so I walked away to cool off."

"And when you returned, what did you find?"

Trent closed his eyes for a second. "Briar with another guy."

"That must have annoyed you even more."

Trent consulted with his mother. "Not really. I was already thinking of ending things, but didn't want to ruin the fun. I figured I could make it through the festival and then bail on her."

"Did Briar find out that was your plan?" Cythera asked.

"She didn't have a clue. I don't want to be involved in any of this. I just want to go home."

"Even though you and Briar were having trouble, you don't want to know what happened to her?" Finn said.

"I... I mean, sure. But Briar wasn't my girlfriend. We weren't serious. It was casual fun. I need to get home and forget about this."

"Why do you need to leave so quickly?" Cythera said.

Trent chewed on his thumbnail. "I don't want my family dragged into this. It would devastate them."

"Your family?" Finn glanced at his mother.

Trent did the same, shame in his eyes. "I'm married with two young children."

"That's charming!" Zandra said. "Trent's a cheat and a liar."

"I'm assuming your wife doesn't know you came to this festival with Briar?" Cythera said.

"She'd kill me if she knew. And she'd get me fired. I work in corporate banking, and her father is my boss. If any of this gets back to her, I'm ruined."

"He's already ruined," Zandra muttered. "What a scummy person."

"Why did you run when my... consultant wanted to question you at the festival?" Cythera said.

"I was trying to get away before I got dragged into this investigation," Trent said. "I had to protect my family and my career. They're the most important things to me."

"He should have thought about that before he cheated on his wife," I said. "This information gives Trent an even stronger motive. Perhaps Briar threatened to reveal his dirty little secret to his wife, so he had to silence her."

"Where did your wife think you were going this weekend?" Cythera said.

"To a banking convention. She finds my job boring, so never asks questions when I tell her I have to go to a conference." Trent clasped his hands together. "I need to get home, or she'll be suspicious. I told her the conference ended today."

"He's still looking out for himself," Zandra said. "Trent doesn't care Briar is dead."

"My client had nothing to do with Miss Vixen's death. Although he is deeply regretful this happened to her, he wasn't involved. And he has an alibi," Trent's mother said.

"What would that be?" Cythera said.

Trent's expression brightened. "I was in the middle of the second color dash. Loads of people saw me."

"And your autopsy results have revealed Briar was drained by two puncture wounds that were made on her neck. My understanding is, you have a vampire in custody who confessed to the crime," Trent's mother said smoothly. "So there's no logical reason you should still consider my client a suspect."

Cythera adjusted her position. "Despite having a confession, we have a right to investigate all suspects. Your client was in a relationship with the victim. They were seen arguing not long before her death, and, as your client succinctly revealed, he has a good reason to want to keep Briar quiet about his affair."

Trent's mother remained unmoved as Cythera laid out the details. "Check your facts before you make accusations. My client was in a public space surrounded by other people. He was nowhere near Miss Vixen when her life was taken. And with the tenuous motive you put forward, you can't hold him any longer."

"If we were in that room, we'd be hearing Cythera grinding her teeth," I said.

"She'd be right to grind," Zandra said. "The mother is fiercely defending her cub, even though that cub is a jerk."

After a few more moments of discussion, it was clear Trent wouldn't supply any useful information, so Cythera wound up the questioning and left Trent and his mother in the interview room.

Finn came into our room and closed the door behind him. "That didn't get us far, other than making Cythera angry."

"Trent has got a great motive for murder," I said.

"He has, but we can't hold him. And with Valentine still confessing to Briar's murder, our hands are tied. We'll check Trent's alibi, but if it reveals he was at the color dash, then we have to rule him out as a suspect."

Zandra sighed. "So, what do we do next?"

"We get to animal control," I said. "Otherwise, Barney will think we've resigned without telling him."

Zandra checked the time and jumped to her feet. "We're late! Meet you back here after work?"

Finn nodded. "If we get a break in the case, I'll let you know. Otherwise, see you later."

***

Following a busy day at animal control, we returned to Angel Force to regroup and review the case. Cythera was there, along with Finn and Bertoli. She didn't seem impressed we'd joined them, but made no comment, other than heaving a sigh and fluttering her wings.

"We've come to a standstill in this investigation." Cythera stood beside a whiteboard with the suspects names and details written on. "We have a number of suspects, one of whom is confessing to

Briar's murder, but without solid evidence, we can't bring a prosecution against him. Yet."

"Yay for Valentine," I whispered.

Cythera looked at the group of assembled angels. "So, where to go from here?"

"If you want my expert opinion, you only have to ask," I said.

Cythera held a finger to her lips. "Not you. We have Valentine, one of Remus's hive vampires, who is determined to make us believe he's guilty."

"But he was vague during his interview and couldn't provide any detail about being with Briar," I said. "He couldn't remember anything about her. Which is odd, since he spent time draining her."

Cythera glanced at me. "Correct. We can all agree he's covering for Remus."

"We don't agree with that," Zandra said. "Valentine thinks he's covering for Remus, but Remus has nothing to hide."

Cythera arched an eyebrow. "Remus concealed he knew the victim and fought with her just before she died."

"Because he was concerned it would make him look guilty," I said. "And you've just proven that concern correct."

"Remus's handkerchief was in the victim's hand," Cythera said. "It didn't get there by magic. And there are two puncture wounds on her neck."

"You really think it was Remus?" I asked.

Cythera gently flared her nostrils. "I have my suspicions about him. He's top of my list. Moving on, we have Trent Masters."

"Who was about to make a run for it. And he's sneaky," I said.

"Unfortunately, there's little we can do about that now. Not with his mother guarding him."

"Have you checked his alibi yet?" Zandra said.

"Soon. We'll ask around when we return to Remus's." Cythera tapped the board. "We also have Keanu Sweeny."

"A shifty creeper who stalked Briar and lied about fighting over her," I said.

"He's still a suspect. Just like Trent, we need witnesses who saw him at the color dash. If no one can confirm he was there, then he remains a suspect, too."

"What about Briar's sisters?" Zandra said.

"Primrose has an alibi. Dahlia doesn't. We've yet to find anyone who saw her, so she must remain a suspect as well."

"Dahlia said she was on her own," I said. "Did she lie?"

"Possibly. For now, I'm focused on the vampires. I'm waiting for a search warrant to come through for Remus's mansion. Once I have that, we'll head there and ask around."

"Why search Remus's mansion?" I asked. "He didn't do this."

Cythera fluttered her wings. "That's for me to determine. In the meantime, we need more background information on all suspects. Let's find out if any of them are hiding significant information."

"Like a wife, a corporate banking job, and two children?" I said.

"Exactly! Let's get to work." Cythera barked orders and sent her angels scurrying to do background research on the remaining suspects.

She headed to her office, and I hopped onto Zandra's shoulder. "We need to warn Remus what's about to go down. He won't appreciate a group of angels descending on his home and pulling it apart because Cythera has a chip on her shoulder."

Zandra winced. "She'll be furious if she catches us meddling, but we should say something. Remus won't want to get caught with his pants down." As she spoke, she sidled toward the exit, only pausing to grab pictures of Trent and Keanu off a desk.

"Remus needs to know what's coming his way. He'd do the same for us if he knew Angel Force was about to descend on our basement and snoop through your underwear drawer."

Zandra hesitated, then nodded, and pulled open the door. Archie sat outside.

"What are you doing here?" I said. "Shouldn't you be keeping Remus company?"

Archie looked away and lowered his muzzle. "I came for an update. Remus is stressed, so I thought if I found out what was going on, it would make him happy."

"You were snooping?" Zandra shooed him away from the door so she could step outside.

"I'm worried about Remus. He's sad." Archie loped beside us.

"Does that mean you were snooping?" I hopped off Zandra's shoulder as we headed away from the building.

"Not to do harm. You know I'm a good boy."

"And you'll always look after Remus, no matter what he gets himself into," Zandra said. "You're a loyal hound, but don't get into trouble because of him."

"I'll defend Remus's honor to the end. He's a good vampire, too. He just sometimes forgets." Archie lifted his head. "I'll prove to you he's good. Come with me, and you'll see how amazing he is."

"We were headed that way to give him a heads up about what the angels have planned," I said. "What's he up to?"

"He's holding a memorial for Briar. You should see the place. It's like a Gothic movie set got married to the Nightmare Before Christmas."

"That doesn't sound good. Let's get in the van, and I'll put my foot down," Zandra said. "We need to do damage limitation before Angel Force get there."

Fifteen minutes later, we were parked at Remus's mansion. I stared open-mouthed at the scene before us. Black candles glimmered, huge orbs of sparkling light drifted around the grounds, and there was an intense waft of incense drifting in the air. There were also open coffins propped on rocks, draped in black velvet. Sad rock music blared from hidden speakers.

I climbed out of the van and hurried along with Zandra and Archie, taking it all in. There were even skeletons posed in various compromising positions.

Remus stood by the front door of his mansion, dressed head to toe in black, his eyes heavily lined with black guyliner and a black velvet top hat perched on his blond hair.

"Remus, what are you up to?" I said.

He spread his arms wide. "I'm mourning! Cythera wants to see how devastated I am by recent events, so I'll give her a ceremony she'll never forget. When are the angels arriving to see the show?"

Chapter 16

Gothic cliches

I narrowed my eyes at the black-clad vampire. "How do you know Cythera is still suspicious of you?"

Remus lifted one shoulder. "I have a loyal vampire in custody, a remarkable hellhound who never lets me down, and friends inside Angel Force. I'm always kept well informed if my liberty is at risk."

Archie hurried over to Remus and leaned his head against his thigh. "Did I do good?"

"You're always an excellent hound." Remus stroked Archie's ears.

"You were listening to the angels' conversations?" I said to Archie.

He whined. "Not deliberately. I came to get an update. I just overheard something interesting, so I kept listening."

"How did you get the news back to Remus so quickly?" Zandra said.

"My dearest witchling in the woods. In case you didn't know, some vampires can turn into bats," Remus said. "I never leave Archie unaccompanied for long, in case some uncouth creature attempts to take him from me."

"Archie has a vampire bodyguard?" I asked.

"When the occasion calls for it. His loyal guard swooped away and informed me of the unsettling situation." Remus waggled his fingers in the air. "But I was already planning this. I just added extra touches to ensure Cythera would get a delightful surprise when she arrived."

"The coffins are a bit much," I said.

"Some might even say crass," Zandra said. "Same goes for the skeletons."

"I had some spare coffins in the cellar. Thought they'd be useful. And they're comfortable. Silk lined with pillows. You're welcome to try one, Juno."

"Another time," I said. "What do the partygoers think about having a memorial in the middle of their revelry?"

"They're thrilled to take part. And they're all getting involved and dressing up to look impressively mournful. Even Briar's sisters are happy for the event to take place. They borrowed clothing from me so they can be suitably attired. Look, they're over there." Remus pointed through the crowd at Dahlia and Primrose.

Primrose wore an oversized black shirt, cinched at the waist with a large black belt. Her legs were bare. Primrose wore slightly too large pants, a black T-shirt, and a top hat that had slipped over her ears so you could barely see her eyes.

"They thought this was a good idea?" Zandra said.

"They want to remember their dear sister," Remus said. "Besides, what else can they do while the angels stumble around and attempt to find a solution? I trust you're still steering them in the right direction?"

"When we can. And Dahlia is still a murder suspect," I murmured.

"All the more reason to keep her here and occupied with this event," Remus said. "Who else is on your list?"

"You're still Cythera's prime suspect," I said. "She's arranging a search warrant so she can take apart the mansion."

He grimaced. "What is she expecting to uncover? I have no secrets hidden in my closets. Well, one or two, but they're more of the bedroom variety secret. I shall enjoy seeing Cythera blush when she uncovers those treats."

"This is so bizarre," Zandra muttered, her gaze on two partygoers dressed as giant crows.

"If you're staying, you need to change," Remus said. "We're starting soon. Once the sun is completely down, the celebrations, I mean, the solemn mourning, can begin."

"What have you got planned?" I asked.

"We're starting with some readings. Some of Briar's favorite music will be played. Also, a candlelit walk. And her sisters have agreed to talk about her. I believe Primrose said she'd read song lyrics and Dahlia a poem. It sounds charming. But you must change into something appropriately dour so you can take part, too."

"I'm keeping my fur white," I said.

"And I'm not changing out of my jeans," Zandra said. "We're here to work."

"Are you sure? You'd make a beautiful black cat, Juno," Remus said. "I can't tempt you to step into the fluffy dark side?"

"Positive. And while we're here, we need to ask around to see if Briar's boyfriend, Trent, and a guy who was stalking her have alibis."

"Good. More suspects to get me off the hook. Ask your questions before the mourning begins, though. I don't want you ruining the solemnity." Remus rubbed his hands together and grinned. He was so melodramatic.

We got busy showing around Trent and Keanu's pictures. It took a while, but we discovered people who'd seen them at the color dash.

Zandra slid the pictures into her pocket and sighed. "Two suspects ruled out just like that. This doesn't look good for the vampires."

"What are you doing?" Primrose approached us, holding Dahlia's hand. "I heard you're asking questions about Trent."

I jumped onto Zandra's shoulder, so I could be eye level with the Vixen sisters. "Greetings! We're still investigating what happened to your sister."

"I'll tell you what happened. A dumb vampire bit her," Primrose said. "I'm no super sleuth, but even I know what went down. Everyone is saying it was a vampire."

"Not everyone," Dahlia murmured. "People are wondering if something else happened to her."

Primrose fluffed her blonde hair. "Like what? She fell on a garden fork? Nothing else could have left those holes in her neck. It was a classic vampire attack. And I even heard a vamp confessed. If that's true, why are you still asking about Trent?"

"To make sure we have the right person," I said. "Surely, you wouldn't want her killer to get away with it, would you?"

Primrose scowled. "You really think Trent was involved? I was sure it was a vampire."

"All the vampires here seem nice," Dahlia said. "And they've been charming to us. The one who owns this house said we could stay here until things get resolved."

Primrose folded her arms across her chest. "Of course, I said there was no way we'd stay here. If we did, we'd be their next victims."

"Remus has been kind to us," Primrose said. "He said whatever we needed, we just had to ask. He even helped with our mourning outfits. These pants he loaned me are Gucci. I've never worn anything designer. They're so soft."

"You look ridiculous," Primrose said. "You should have borrowed a shirt, like I did."

"I don't have the legs to pull off that look." Dahlia blinked at us from behind her glasses, a sad smile on her face. "Have you got any news? Have the angels figured out what happened to Briar?"

"We're making progress. And some suspects have been discounted," Zandra said.

"And the vampires?"

"At the moment, one vampire is being held."

"I knew it! Remus kept reassuring us none of his vampires would do this, and they're all well trained and blah, blah, blah, but we know the truth about vampires," Primrose said. "I could never understand why Briar was so obsessed with them. Real vampires are nothing like the movie vampires. They're cold, vicious, and soulless. They see us as food and just want to drain our blood. I heard a rumor they love witches' blood because it's so sweet."

"You must mean angel blood. It has a cinnamon sugar taste," I said. "And there are doubts about the vampire's credibility. That's why we're continuing to investigate."

Primrose stared at the mansion. "I wish we'd never come here."

"Why did you come to the Blood Moon Festival if you dislike vampires so much?" I asked.

"What other option did I have? Stay home and be bored while Briar and Dahlia have all the fun?" Primrose shook her head. "Never going to happen. And think how bad things would have gotten if I wasn't here? Dahlia would keep fainting and crying. I'm holding this family together."

Dahlia sighed, but made no comment.

"Remus was telling us about the memorial event for Briar. You're involved?" I asked.

"I don't want to be. It doesn't seem right, supporting what the vampires do when one of them drained Briar," Primrose said.

"We're involved." Dahlia slid Primrose a glare. "And it's sweet of them to do this. If we'd held a memorial service back home, I doubt many people would have come. We don't even have neighbors close to where we live. We're out in the sticks."

"They wouldn't come even if they lived close. Briar was always mean to the Griswalds when she drove past their house. It would have been us standing in a cold hall staring at her coffin. What a grim thought," Primrose said.

"So, you approve of what the bloodthirsty killer vampires have done for Briar?" I cocked my head.

Primrose scowled at me and looked away. "I guess I don't hate it. And there's supposed to be fireworks later. Maybe they're not so terrible. Some of them are cute."

"It's so kind of them to help us," Dahlia said. "With everyone here, we can remember Briar, share stories about her, and give her a proper send off. She loved to party, so this is a perfect goodbye." Her eyes filled with tears.

"Don't start blubbing again. It's boring, and you never cry pretty." Primrose looked at me and Zandra. "If you really think it wasn't a vampire, then it's good you're hunting Trent."

"Why Trent?" I said.

"I don't trust him."

"You don't trust anybody," Dahlia said.

"Why should I? And he's too good-looking, thinks all the ladies want him. He made a pass at me when he started seeing Briar! I had to fight him off, and he turned mean because I said no."

Dahlia looked startled. "Primrose! That's not how I remember things."

"You weren't there, so you don't know what happened."

Dahlia dropped her gaze to the dirt. "True, but you told me what happened, and you never said—"

"You're remembering it wrong, as usual. Trent is sleazy. And I'm sure he was hiding something from

Briar." Primrose leaned closer, a gleam in her eyes as she bad-mouthed Trent. "Sometimes, when he was with her, he'd get messages and scurry off to look at them. And he had two mobile snow globes. I asked him about it, and he said one was for work and the other for personal use."

"Trent does have a secret. He revealed it when Angel Force questioned him," I said. "But he also has an alibi. We've established he was in the color dash when Briar was killed."

"Oh! You're sure?" Primrose's bottom lip jutted out. "It would teach him a lesson, thinking he could have his cake and eat it. He probably got off on the thought of seeing sisters at the same time. Creep."

"That's a horrible thing to say," Dahlia said. "Trent is a little smooth, but he always paid me attention. He was nice to me and asked me questions. Few guys do that."

"He was nice to you because he felt sorry for you," Primrose said. "When you weren't around, he called you the perfect little spinster."

"Don't be nasty. He never said that."

Primrose sneered at her. "Trent spoke to you because you made great cakes. He only wanted you for your food."

The color drained from Dahlia's face as she pushed her glasses up the bridge of her nose. "If you'll excuse me." She hurried away, but not before I saw tears on her cheeks.

Primrose groaned. "Ignore her. She's so sensitive. Always blubbing about something."

"Dahlia has a right to be sad," I said. "She just lost a beloved sister."

Primrose waved a hand in the air. "I'm sad, too, but you don't see me crying."

I twitched my whiskers. Maybe Primrose wasn't crying because she was glad Briar was dead.

"Oh, there's Ronaldo. He promised to buy me a drink and read my aura before the memorial." Primrose hurried away without a backward glance.

"I feel sorry for Dahlia," I said. "Stuck with those two as her only companions, she can't have had much fun. Primrose is a horror, saying those mean things."

"Yeah. Why do that? It's spiteful," Zandra said.

"Because Primrose thinks she's better than Dahlia, but I know who I'd pick to hang out with."

Zandra looked at the growing crowd of mourners dressed in black. "At least we've eliminated Trent and Keanu from our pool of suspects."

"Which isn't great news for Remus and his vampires. Maybe while we've been here, Cythera has uncovered something new. Something that'll point us toward a new suspect."

"We still have Dahlia," Zandra said. "Other than Remus, she's the only one without an alibi."

"She's too sweet to be a killer."

"Aren't they the ones we're supposed to suspect? The suspects too good to be true?"

"Cynic. Let's find Remus. Make sure he's not hauling too many skeletons from his closets to scare Cythera with," I said.

We'd gone a dozen steps before I swiveled my head and inhaled the delectable scent of roasting meat. "They've got triple decker bacon hamburgers! We deserve a five-minute break and a treat since we eliminated two murder suspects."

Zandra's stomach grumbled. "They have that smoked cheddar I like."

"I bet it tastes amazing melted on a triple stack of meat. We can share one. You have the cheese and bun, and I'll have the rest."

She smirked. "We can stop for a few minutes. But we're not sharing."

The queue took a while to move, but within ten minutes, we were munching on greasy hamburgers and gooey melted cheese.

"Any sign of Remus?" Zandra said around a mouthful of burger.

"We should try inside," I said. "He's probably putting the finishing touches to his mourning outfit."

We headed to the main entrance, but there was a large crowd surging around several vampires who were handing out black candles and sparklers. After some pushing and shoving, we gave up trying to get through and stood at the back, finishing our food.

"Let's try around the side," I said.

We walked around the mansion, moving away from the noise and bustle. It was dark, and although the Blood Moon was almost full, the shadows were dense and deep, giving the grounds an eerie vibe.

There was a gentle female giggle, followed by a long, slow sigh.

"Someone's enjoying themselves," I muttered.

"Hardly a surprise. Everyone is high on magic and the joys of life. That makes people drop their inhibitions."

I peered through a hole in a clump of shrubbery. Dahlia was being held by a tall, blond vampire, and he was about to sink his fangs into her neck.

Chapter 17

Bite me!

"Hey! Stop that." I leaped through the gap in the hedge. My paws hit the ground, and I thundered toward the vampire before he could plunge his fangs into Dahlia's vulnerable neck.

The vampire's head shot up and he hissed at me, his eyes black. It was the Brad Pitt lookalike I'd seen looking miserable when slumped on Remus's couch.

I hissed back and fired up my magic. "Step away from your meal."

Zandra was behind me, a blaze of magic on her fingertips as we grew near to the pair.

The vampire thrust Dahlia behind him, and she hit the ground, giving a squeak of surprise as she tumbled. He bared his fangs. "This is none of your business."

"I disagree. We know Dahlia. Let her go," I said.

He snarled again and coiled.

Before he could attack, I hurled a volley of magic spells at him, my feline senses screaming that this vampire meant business, and if I didn't take him down, he'd be biting me and my witch next.

He roared his anger and surprise as my magic sparked around him, his eyes glinting with an otherworldly light.

With a hiss, I unleashed my magic again, ready for whatever this vampire had in store for me.

Zandra was crouched, sparkling magic swirling in her palm. "Dahlia! Move! Get over here."

Dahlia hid her face in her hands and shook her head.

I circled the vampire, keen to draw him away from Dahlia, my paws glowing with arcane energy. My magic felt stronger than it had done in decades. Strong but unstable. I had to be careful not to unleash power I couldn't control.

The vampire threw himself at me, and I launched a cascade of fiery spells. But he was quick and agile, dodging and weaving with ease, getting closer by the second.

"Dahlia is mine!" he yelled, nearly catching me. "You won't take her from me."

Zandra flung a spell and it whacked him between the shoulder blades, sending him off course and flailing into a bush.

"We need to neutralize this vamp," she said. "He's out of control."

"No!" Dahlia whimpered. "Don't hurt him."

"He must be strong to still have control over her." I stalked toward the fallen vampire, the air crackling with my magic that combined with my witch's power to make us even more potent.

He rolled onto his back, his fangs extended and hatred burning in his eyes.

Dahlia scrambled closer, her pants getting muddy as she slid along the ground. "Stop! I promise, he wasn't hurting me."

"You would say that," I growled out. "He has you in his thrall. He was about to ravage you."

"I can explain." Dahlia scuffled over on her hands and knees. "It's not what you think."

"Zandra, deal with Dahlia. She'll have no control over herself while this vampire has her under his influence," I said. "I must obliterate this creature."

"Don't! Please! I'm begging you," Dahlia said.

A cloud of black smoke engulfed us, and a few seconds later, Remus appeared. He straightened his top hat and arched one eyebrow. "Juno, why are you molesting one of my vampires?" Although his tone was level, his eyes sparked with anger and his fangs were visible.

"He was about to devour Dahlia," I said. "He has no control over his primal urges. If we hadn't intervened, Dahlia would be dead. Most likely drained, just like her sister."

"Galahad, were you involving yourself with this delightful young woman without her consent?" Remus asked the vampire, who remained in the dirt.

"No! This is a misunderstanding. Dahlia's happy to be with me. We're dating."

There was a second of surprised silence as we stared at Galahad.

"Check Dahlia's pupils to see if Galahad's compelled her," I said.

Zandra did as instructed. "She looks good. Do you know Galahad?"

Dahlia nodded. "And... I wasn't brought here against my will."

"I believe you two are already acquainted," Remus said.

A flush rose up Dahlia's throat and onto her cheeks. "I met Galahad when we got to the festival. We hit it off straight away. He saw I was upset just now and came to comfort me."

I eased back the spell that held down the vampire. "You weren't about to take a drink from her?"

"Of course not. I saw her crying and wanted to help. As soon as we met, I found her charming. Different to the other women here. Modest, sweet, and intelligent. If anything, she beguiled me."

Dahlia stifled a smile behind one hand. "I couldn't believe it when Galahad picked me. Briar and Primrose are stunning. I've always been the plain sister, the one the guys overlook, unless they're using me to get to my sisters. But Galahad wasn't like that. He came straight to me and he couldn't stop staring. And we talked for hours."

"And kissed." Galahad smiled at Dahlia. "I remember every one of your beautiful kisses."

"Sounds intense," Zandra muttered. "Are you sure you're not feeling the aftereffects of his thrall? It can take a while to shake off if the vampire is strong."

"I promise, I'm not. I know what I'm saying." Dahlia climbed to her feet and brushed dirt off her borrowed pants. "And... I was with Galahad the first night, too. The night Briar was killed."

"You lied about having an alibi?" I asked.

"Why conceal that from the angels?" Zandra said. "You made yourself a murder suspect for no reason."

Dahlia cast her gaze down. "Because I didn't want my reputation tarnished. What would people think if they knew I was making out with a hot vampire while my sister was being killed? I should have been protecting her, not forgetting myself in Galahad's arms."

"That's what you were doing that night?" Primrose stomped over, her eyes wide and eyebrows raised. "I can't believe you lied to me! You always scold me for dating different guys and bringing them home when I barely know them. But here you are, making nasty with the undead, when you should have been stopping our sister from being drained."

"Let's not be too hasty." I backed away from Galahad, issuing him a warning glare not to try anything. "My apologies for almost obliterating you. You must understand how the situation appeared when we discovered you smooching."

He rolled to his feet. "It's fine. You were looking out for Dahlia, so I can only thank you for your swift actions. I'd do anything to keep her safe. She's magnificent."

Remus grinned. "Would you now, my dear friend? Has one of my hive fallen in love with a warm blood?"

Galahad flinched. "I know it's not approved of, but look at her. And if you spend time with Dahlia, you'll learn how she captivated me. She's the most incredible woman I've ever met."

"You can't be serious." Primrose crossed her arms over her chest. "This is a joke."

"I'm deadly serious. I adore Dahlia. I'm in love with her."

"You... you love me!" Dahlia took a step back.

Galahad clasped her hand in his. "The second I heard your sweet voice, I knew you were special. And after spending so much time with you, I can't imagine not seeing you every day."

"Easy, my friend," Remus said softly. "The living don't feel as intensely as we do. You don't want to frighten your new love."

"Dahlia will grow to love me as much as I do her. I've found the woman I want to spend the rest of my life with."

"Oh! That's sweet. I'm excessively fond of you, too." Dahlia's cheeks were so flushed, I grew concerned about her blood pressure. "But I need time. This is all very sudden."

"He's really that good?" Primrose said, her expression morphing from jealous harpy to curious crow. "Maybe I need to change my mind about vampires if this blood sucker has got you so flustered."

Dahlia ignored her sister. She looked at Galahad and her flush of joy faded, along with her stunned smile. "No. I'm sorry. I can't be with you."

His expression dropped. "Why not? We're perfect for each other."

"I don't disagree. You're gorgeous, funny, great to be around, and you make me feel amazing about myself."

"I sense a but coming," I said.

Dahlia nodded. "I have a reputation to maintain."

"What reputation?" Primrose said.

"My career."

"As a boring part-time librarian," Primrose shrieked. "You're so tedious and uptight about your books."

"They're not just any old books. I'm a custodian of rare plant magic books," Dahlia said. "I worked hard to get that position."

"I don't know why you bother. It's a waste of time. You get below minimum wage and they work you until you're exhausted." Primrose shook her head. "It's not as if you need to work. We have money."

"I do it because I want to work there. It gives me a purpose," Dahlia said. "I couldn't follow my passion for art, but I love my time at the library, cataloguing rare finds and helping people who love books as much as I do."

"I adore books, too." Galahad's expression brightened. "I could show you the library here. It's magnificent. It'll keep you occupied for the rest of your days."

"I do have a wonderful collection of first editions," Remus said. "Some are even signed by the author. You're welcome to inspect the collection."

Dahlia's eyes widened. Then she caught herself and shook her head. "The institution I work for has old-fashioned values. They only employ people whose reputations are beyond reproach."

Primrose smirked. "You should tell them about your hot new relationship. You never know, they may think you're cool for fornicating with a vampire and give you a pay raise."

"Oh! No! We didn't fornicate." Dahlia fanned her face with her free hand.

"If you want fornication, I'd be thrilled to oblige," Galahad said. "Whatever makes you happy. I just want to spend time with you."

"How charming." Remus's eyes sparkled with amusement. "I've created a vampire with the machinations of a romantic poet. Just to confirm, although I already had my suspicions, you were together the evening of the murder?"

"Yes. We were together when Briar died." Galahad pressed a hand over his heart. "You have my word."

Remus stared unblinking at Galahad, then smiled. "That nicely resolves matters. I need a drink after this adventure. Does anyone else need a drink? I have all the blood types. Chilled or warm."

While the group talked about their preferred blood of choice and Galahad cooed over Dahlia, I leaped onto Zandra's shoulder and sniffed her ear. "That rules out another suspect. Which means the only one left is Remus."

Chapter 18

Biting puzzle

After the adventures of fighting a vampire and discounting another suspect, we needed a break. We settled in Remus's opulent powder blue themed supper room, a delectable spread of tea and crumpets with a variety of sweet preserves set out for everyone. Well, not the vampires, so the feast was for Zandra. And she was happily tucking in. Using her magic always made her hungry.

Dahlia and Primrose had chosen not to join us, and had left to talk about dating vampires, and were no doubt dissecting Galahad's startling declaration of love.

"Perhaps the A Positive 1862 French Riviera blend would improve your mood." Remus crouched in front of Galahad, who was slumped in a seat, his head in his hands.

"I can make her happy. I know I can."

Remus patted Galahad's knee. "Sometimes, warm bloods don't know a good thing when it's in front of them. You'd make Dahlia a wonderful companion. She'd want for nothing if she was under your care."

"And we could be together forever." Galahad lifted his head. "With your permission, I'd like to offer her the chance of immortality."

"Shouldn't you try a committed relationship with Dahlia before you turn her?" I said. "Immortality isn't to be stepped into lightly. A cute habit could make you grind your teeth a hundred years from now. You need to think long term."

He moaned softly. "If I offer her that gift, it may make Dahlia want me. I have to make her love me."

I gently cleared my throat. "You shouldn't need to offer incentives or bribes to get someone to be with you. Dahlia is level-headed. She's had to be the sensible one in the family since her parents died. Give her time to figure things out."

Galahad looked at me. "Do you think she'll consider my proposal?"

"I'm sure she'll consider what a life with a vampire would be like before making any rash decisions."

"But she chose books over me!" His head lowered. "I thought we had something. Dahlia's so different from the other women here. Respectable. Kind. Sweet."

Remus stood, one hand resting lightly on Galahad's shoulder. "After a few pints of premium A Positive from my cellar, you'll forget Dahlia."

"I'll never forget her. She's what I've been looking for. A neat, tidy female, with solid values. Proper values."

Remus caught my eye and shrugged. "Galahad comes from a time when values were different."

"When the mere flash of a bare ankle caused men's hearts to race and marriage proposals to drop?" I said.

"You get the idea. Dahlia has a certain innocent charm that would appeal to many."

"She must take her reputation seriously, since she was willing to be a suspect in her sister's murder rather than reveal the truth about your assignation," I said.

"Maybe take that as a sign to move on." Zandra shoved half a crumpet in her mouth.

"You're wrong. It's a sign I haven't tried enough."

"My dear boy. You sound on the verge of obsession, and that's an unattractive quality to offer any woman." Remus paced in front of Galahad. "I have a solution. It's time you took a break from your duties. I'm sending you away."

Galahad's head shot up. "You can't! I must be with Dahlia. If I'm not around her, she'll forget me. Someone else will capture her heart and I'll lose her forever."

"Dahlia will leave here soon," I said. "She'll return home with her sister once Briar's murder is solved."

"She'll get on with her life, and you can get on with yours." Another chunk of crumpet entered Zandra's mouth.

"I don't want her to leave." Galahad looked up at Remus. "Can we keep her here?"

"Holding warm bloods against their will only get the angels tapping on our door and asking awkward questions. We've had enough of those. A trip abroad is what you need," Remus said. "A monastic center in Rome has caught my interest. They operate at night, so I'm thinking it's a clandestine vampire hive. I'd be interested in learning more. I'll arrange the details, and you can leave next week."

Galahad grumbled to himself, but didn't disobey an order from his master.

There was a knock at the door, and a second later it was opened and Finn was shown in.

He nodded at everyone. "Hey. Someone camping outside reported a commotion. Is everything good?"

"More than good. We've successfully discounted a number of suspects," I said. "Dahlia wasn't on her own when Briar was murdered. She was with this fine vampire."

Finn's eyebrows rose, and he nodded. "What were you two doing together?"

I chuckled. "What do lusty young couples usually do when they're together?"

"Oh! Got you." Finn stifled a grin. "And since you borrowed pictures of Trent and Keanu before leaving Angel Force, I guess you checked their alibis too. Any results?"

Zandra finished her crumpet and licked strawberry preserves off her fingers. "We decided not to wait for Cythera to get the search warrant and cause chaos."

"More like you wanted to warn your friend we were coming for him." Finn glanced at Remus. "No hard feelings. This isn't personal. But if I was in charge, I'd be coming for you, too. We're running out of suspects."

Remus hissed softly. "As unhappy as that news makes me, I understand your course of action. It's foolish, but I see how the evidence you've gathered points my way."

"Do we have any new suspects?" I hopped onto the couch next to Zandra. "Has the background research you've been doing found anyone new to investigate?"

Finn shook his head. "Nothing has popped. Cythera's not happy."

After a brief biscuit making session, I settled on a plump blue cushion. "Keanu and Trent were seen at the color dash, so that discounts them. Dahlia was with Galahad. Primrose was dancing topless at the color dash, as numerous starry-eyed witnesses confirmed. That only leaves us with..." I looked at Remus.

He hummed under his breath for a second. "I won't deny it looks bad for me. I concealed my fight with Briar, and she was found with my handkerchief clasped in her hand."

"And let's not forget the vampire bites on her neck," I said.

"It's no one from my hive," Remus said. "I would know. I spoke to each of them to be certain."

"What about the vampire we're still holding?" Finn said. "Valentine confessed he killed Briar."

"He's doing that to protect me. If I could speak to Valentine, I'd convince him to recant his confession. It was a loyal move, but not smart, since it muddied the waters of your investigation and made it appear as if I ordered him to confess, making me look guilty."

"It wasn't him," Galahad said. "He was with the rest of us that night."

Remus startled and turned slowly on one heel. "Why haven't you told me this?"

Galahad looked shame-faced. "Valentine is determined to protect the hive, and that means keeping you free to rule. We all agreed a sacrifice had to be made."

Remus was silent, one hand stroking the front of his pressed shirt. "You can't think I murdered that woman?"

"Never! But when we heard how she died, we knew Angel Force would think one of us was guilty. And when your silk hankie was found... we just had to keep you safe."

"Valentine stepped up as the guilty party, so the rest of you could remain free," I said.

Galahad nodded. "We were all willing to do it, but he was the most insistent."

"Loyal till the end. Foolish, wonderful creature." Remus turned to Finn. "You see. All of my vampires are innocent. Although I will have words with them regarding forming alliances behind my back."

"Only to protect you!" Galahad said. "For the good of the hive."

Remus rested a hand on Galahad's shoulder. "I decide what is best for my hive. But your loyalty is always appreciated."

I turned in a circle and settled back down. "We keep coming up against the immovable problem of the bite. Something bit and drained Briar."

"Yes, that is odd," Remus said. "It would help if I could see her body. I'm well-versed in vampire bites, having administered many over the decades.

If I could look, I may be able to tell if there's anything odd about the holes."

Finn shook his head. "With Valentine off the hook, you're our only suspect. Cythera won't let you anywhere near Briar's body."

"She must see sense and realize I'm not involved. And surely, the search warrant threat is simply that. Cythera is hoping it'll unnerve me and I'll say something foolish to implicate myself."

"Cythera is flapping, stuck for a solution, and an eleven on the grumpy scale. She means business. She's not playing around. She'll get that warrant," Finn said.

"I've noticed she's been grumpier than usual," I said. "Any reason?"

"No one knows. But it means she's digging her heels in with this case. She sees a bite that looks vampire made, so assumes a vampire murdered Briar. It's not an illogical thought."

"Simply an incorrect one," Remus said.

"There was something strange about the bite wound," I said. "The holes weren't neat, as if the vampire had trouble getting hold of Briar."

"That proves it can't be any of my vampires," Remus said. "We're all skilled feeders."

I nodded. "And if a newly made vampire attacked Briar and struggled to bite her, there'd have been more mess, but the site where she was found was pristine."

"That sounds like the work of one of mine, but even experts spill a little in moments of excitement," Remus said.

"We're widening the search area," Finn said. "It's looking likely Briar was killed somewhere else and left in the woods to confuse the situation."

"It's worked," I said. "Since we've nowhere to turn."

No one spoke for a moment. We were stuck as to where to go next.

"If it's any help to your investigation, I'll cancel the rest of the festival," Remus said. "I was considering having an extended after party. It wouldn't be so grand as my original plans, but it would ensure people could enjoy themselves during this remarkable time."

"How about cancelling the memorial for Briar?" I asked.

Remus tugged on his jacket cuff. "People need a place to grieve."

"I don't disagree, but dial it down a dozen notches. The open coffins, fake headstones, all the candles are too..."

"Too crass?"

"I agree with Juno," Finn said. "I wondered what I was walking into. And if that stuff is here when Cythera arrives with the warrant, it'll give her another reason to be angry. She'll think you're using Briar's murder as an excuse to party."

"Who needs an excuse to party?" Remus lifted a hand. "I'll see what I can do. And if you give me access to Valentine, I'll convince him to withdraw his confession. It'll do no one any good if he's charged with murder and the killer is still out there."

"I'll get you access," Finn said.

Remus settled into a chair. "With fewer outstanding issues, Cythera can focus on the clues and find the killer, rather than prodding at my hive. If she prods too hard, we eventually bite."

"Which is all well and good," I said, "but we have no suspects and an unsolved murder on our paws. Where do we go next?"

Chapter 19

What are we missing?

After a restless night, where I tossed and turned, mulling over the lack of new suspects in Briar's murder, I finally rolled out of bed and shook my fur. I turned and looked at my tail. Still missing.

"Want to do something about that?" Zandra walked down the basement steps, a mug of coffee in her hand. "We've got free time before work. I could see if there's something in the chest to magic back your tail."

"I've tried so many spells, and there's been no hint of it coming back. I didn't realize how much I used my tail until it was gone." I wandered to the chest and waited for Zandra to open the lid. Inside was an assortment of spell books, potions, amulets, charms, and wonderful magical items Zandra's mother, Adrienne, had collected over the years as a gift to her daughter.

Zandra set down her coffee and rifled through the chest. She pulled out a spell book and flipped through it. "There's a spell for returning lost things."

"I've tried that. I've tested dozens of spells until my magic was drained and I felt kitten weak. I didn't get so much as a tingle that my tail was returning." I slumped onto my belly. "Maybe I'm being punished."

Zandra arched an eyebrow. "I thought you did this to yourself by accident."

"I did! Why would I want my tail to vanish? Sometimes, magic is tricksy."

"That's the point of it. You need to know what you're dealing with, otherwise you make a mess of things." Zandra tried a second spell book. "And your magic is unique. You sometimes have so much power simmering on those paws that I don't know where it comes from. And it changes. When we first met, your power felt different."

I glanced up at her. "Because of who I was associating with. Now I'm with you, my magic is pure."

Zandra sat back and rested her head on the wall. "It's not just its flavor. It's the intensity. And there have been a few times when your power has shifted wildly. It felt out of control."

"I can't imagine why that would be." I focused on my paws and licked one as I considered my response. We'd both changed, and would change more as our journey evolved. I had my mission to reclaim my stolen power, and Zandra was still learning how to fill her incredible witch boots with the heady mix of magic that roamed within her.

"I have a feeling you do. One day, you might be prepared to tell me about it." Zandra placed the spell books back in the chest. "For now, I'm content with how things are. If you want to keep your secrets, then keep them. So long as it makes you happy."

I tilted my head. She usually wanted answers from me and kept digging until I distracted her. We were both changing. "I appreciate that. Now, what's the plan for work?"

"We don't have to be at work until ten today. We've got that late evening visit at the Hansen place, so I said to Barney we'd take our extra time this morning. I was thinking we could dig into those weird symbols."

"What about Briar's murder? We still don't have a resolution. I thought about it all night and came up with no useful conclusion."

Zandra sipped her coffee. "I'm not sure we'll get a resolution. I got a message from Finn this morning to say Valentine has been released without charge after Remus spoke to him."

"That's good news."

"Not for Remus. Angel Force will conduct a search of his house this afternoon."

"Cythera is clutching at straws if she thinks he's behind this."

"I don't disagree, but he's the only one left without an alibi. He's powerful, but not perfect."

"We know and trust Remus."

"Just because we like someone, it doesn't mean they're not capable of doing bad things. Look at Acer," Zandra said. "She kept a huge family secret from us after her dad was murdered. It got other people killed."

I pondered this information for a moment. "It's true. We never know what's going on behind closed doors. On the surface, everyone's lives seem happy, but you don't have to dig for long before you see most people live in chaos. They shuffle or slam from one problem to another. They pretend everything is good, but the reality is the opposite."

"And imagine what the world would be like if we all told the truth about that chaos?" Zandra shook her head.

"Liberating?"

"It would feel like a much more twisted place."

"Twisted but honest. People would realize that being weird and messy is normal."

Zandra canted her head to the side. "I don't want to consider Remus a suspect. Maybe he has a deceitful vampire in his ranks, though. One who's fooled all of us. Or he's allowed a rogue vampire to slip through the net. Sometimes, master vamps lose their edge."

I huffed out a gentle snort. "Do you want to lose Remus as a friend by digging into that dirt to find out if any of that is true?"

She drank more coffee, then shrugged. "As you often say, justice has to prevail."

The thought of Remus losing his edge and allowing this crime to take place left me queasy. It wouldn't only injure Remus and his hive, it would devastate Archie, too. He was a sensitive hellhound and a close friend.

"We should let Angel Force tie up the loose ends in this investigation, just in case they lead back to Remus and his hive," Zandra said.

"What if the angels charge an innocent vampire of murder because they're out of other options and Cythera needs a win? The mood she's in, I don't trust her judgment."

"If it gets to that, we'll step back in. How about we take a few hours off of thinking about murder?" Zandra slid a pile of books my way. "I borrowed these from Vorana's store. They could help us figure out what's going on with those symbols."

I regarded the books. "We don't focus on murder, but we focus on strange chaos making gremlins and the possibility my former snuggle buddy is involved with them?"

Zandra winced. "Well, you did say everyone and everything was weird. Let's find out how weird those symbols are."

"We'll get to the symbols soon, but I can't focus on them right now." I stood and paced from one side of the basement to the other. "I keep thinking about the blood. If it wasn't at the scene and a vampire didn't drink it, where is it? You can't easily hide that much blood."

Zandra tucked away the books. "So, what do you want to do?"

"Return to the start. We've overlooked something. We need to go back to the woods."

She gently thumped the back of her head against the wall. "So much for a peaceful start to our day."

"You should thank me. You'd be bored looking through books about archaic symbols."

"I'd do it if it helped you with a puzzle."

I jumped on her lap, placed my front paws on her shoulders, and rested my forehead against hers.

Zandra smiled, then drew back and kissed my head. "Let me finish my coffee, then we'll take a trip to the woods."

Twenty minutes later, we were drawing up outside of Remus's place. All signs of the gothic memorial had vanished, although there were still people camping and even a few food stands operating.

"There's Trent and Keanu," I said to Zandra as we headed toward Remus's mansion.

"And they look friendly. They must have bonded over sharing a dead girlfriend."

I smirked. "And there's Primrose and Dahlia! What are they doing here so early? Last I heard, they were still staying with Sorcha."

"Let's find out." Zandra strode over to them. "Hey! You're not staying at Sorcha's anymore?"

Dahlia looked up, then shook her head. "No, it was good of her to offer, but the café is so noisy all the time. Sorcha's boyfriend was having a big gathering about their future protests, and we couldn't sleep. So, we took Remus up on the offer to stay here."

"I told her it was a dumb idea, and we'd end up getting our throats torn out." Primrose was folding a colored shawl and placing it into a bag.

"It's funny how you stopped complaining when you saw the enormous four poster bed you got," Dahlia murmured. "Remus even gifted her a case of top-of-the-line cosmetics."

"He has a way of finding people's weaknesses," I said. "Have you spoken to Galahad since you've been here?"

A blush chased up Dahlia's neck and onto her cheeks. "We've spoken."

"Are you considering his offer?"

"Of immortality?" Dahlia nodded. "Although it was almost as shocking as his declaration of love. We barely know each other."

"Vampires love deeply and forever if you let them in," I said. "He must see something special in you."

"Why her?" Primrose threw down her bag. "It was Briar who wanted immortality. She was always going on about it. Dahlia's the sensible one who bleats on about eternal life not being so special. But the first chance she gets, she wants to be turned. Such a hypocrite."

"I didn't say I'd accept his offer," Dahlia said. "But I'm wondering if I can combine my books and my vampire boyfriend. We're talking things through. And I do like him."

"Galahad was heartbroken when you turned him down," I said. "Maybe you need a guy who gets obsessed with you and treats you like the goddess you truly are."

"Her! A goddess?" Primrose sneered. "More like a fatted calf ready to be sacrificed to a conniving vampire."

While Zandra chatted to Dahlia and Primrose, I snuck over to Primrose's open bag. I'd had a furball churning in my gut since last night and it was time it came out. Primrose's bag was the perfect place to leave it. The rude little madam deserved a gift she wouldn't forget in a hurry.

After quietly heaving up my furball, then ensuring it was tucked underneath the shawl, I re-joined the conversation.

The ground shook beneath my feet, and I turned to discover Archie bounding toward me. He swooped his enormous tongue at my head, but I avoided an Archie spit bath with a swift sidestep and a bat of his ear with a murder mitten.

He wagged his tail, not minding being swiped by my paw. "How's it going? Any news on the investigation?"

I gestured with my head, then walked away, so we were out of earshot of Primrose and Dahlia. "We're going back to the beginning and starting at the site where we found Briar's body. I want to sniff around and see if anything was overlooked."

"Oh! Sounds good. I can help! I've got an amazing nose. I can smell a raw steak from ten miles away."

"Your nose will be most welcome. And I could do with any spare vampires, too. We're looking for an old bloody trail, so they're the perfect supernatural creatures to find such a thing."

His tail thumped on the ground. "Give me five minutes. I'll round up the vampires and we'll come sniff with you." Archie turned and raced back to the mansion.

We said goodbye to Primrose and Dahlia, and headed toward the woods.

"Archie is bringing back up," I said to Zandra. "I figured we could sniff around and see if any clues are lurking the angels missed."

"I'll leave the sniffing to you," Zandra said.

We headed into the woods and located the site where Briar was found. It was quiet, a gentle breeze whispering the leaves to life and soft birdsong, but other than that, we were alone. For all of two minutes. Half a dozen puffs of smoke, three bat arrivals later, and Archie crashing into the clearing, disturbed the peace. Soon, seven vampires, Archie, me, and Zandra began a search of the area.

We sniffed and hunted, hunted and sniffed, looking for any clue to suggest who had murdered Briar and what they'd done with her blood.

"I've got something." A vampire volunteer stood by the spot where Briar's body had been discovered. "It's just a faint scent, though."

"Briar was left there. Does the scent you've picked up lead anywhere?" I asked.

The vampire walked in a slow circle with his head raised and mouth open. "No. I've got nothing."

"Maybe she was translocated here," Zandra said. "If Briar was killed somewhere else and magic was used to bring her body to the woods, there'd be no physical trail to follow."

I hoped that wasn't the case. Otherwise, this would be a waste of time.

We searched for another half an hour, but no one found any trail to suggest where Briar had been brought from.

"When we're done here, I've got something amazing to show you," Archie whispered to me.

I lifted my head. "What's that?"

"My gift from Remus. It was the surprise he was arranging on the evening Briar was killed."

"There really was a gift?" With the unsettling doubts about Remus still lingering, this was a thread of hope I was thrilled to grab.

"Sure. Remus never lies to me. And what a treat it is. It's one-of-a-kind. The most amazing thing you'll ever see." Archie's long tail whipped against the side of an ancient spruce.

I stopped sniffing, my interest piqued. "What is it?"

"It's a portrait of us. You gotta see it."

I twitched my whiskers. I had a limited appreciation for art. "Perhaps later. I want to do one more circuit of this area. I know we've missed something important. It must be here."

Archie followed me. "It gets better. It's way better than you could ever dream of."

"Does the portrait make you look handsome?"

"Of course! Remus says he has the most handsome hellhound in the world. But it's not that." He nipped my ear and whined. "You're not listening! I want to share this with you."

I stopped and rubbed my ear with a paw. "My apologies. I have a lot on my mind. Tell me all about it."

Archie's ears pricked. "The portrait has a built-in treat dispenser. All I have to do to get a treat is touch my nose to Remus's hand in the portrait, and he dispenses tasty food."

I considered this interesting invention just as my stomach growled. "Zandra, Archie has something to show me in the mansion. We'll be back soon. Keep looking."

She raised her hand as we bounded off to see the portrait. Now food had been included, I was more inclined to take a peek.

"It's a shame no one saw Remus working on your gift that evening," I said. "It would get him in the clear."

"He's already in the clear. None of us think he did it. I know you don't either."

"Of course. But we need evidence of his innocence, since Cythera is still interested in him. And unfortunately, only him."

"You'll clear Remus's name. You always catch the killer. Follow me. The portrait is in the study."

I usually had a solid belief in my abilities, but I was doubting myself in proving Remus's innocence. I didn't want my vampire friend to get in trouble, but when Cythera was backed into a corner, she reacted rashly. And given the foul mood she was in, I wouldn't put it past her to charge Remus just to get this case off her desk.

"What do you think?" Archie stood to the side of an enormous portrait that showed Remus in an immaculate dove gray suit with a matching top hat. Archie was beside him, looking up at Remus proudly, his tongue hanging out.

"It's stunning," I said. "Where's the treat dispenser?"

"Watch this." Archie pressed his nose into Remus's hand and three treats appeared at the bottom of the portrait. "They taste incredible." He nudged one my way and ate the other two.

Archie repeated the exercise several times, and I was soon convinced I needed a portrait of me and

Zandra with built-in treats. It was genius. I could look at my wonderful witch anytime I wanted, while feasting.

"We should head back outside and join the others," I said. "It was my idea to sniff for clues, so I can't abandon them."

Archie gobbled one final treat, and then we left the study. We were heading along the corridor when a quiet voice filtered out of a room. I poked my head inside and spotted several half-asleep vampires slumped on couches or chairs.

"What you doing?" Archie whispered. "I thought you wanted to go outside."

"In a minute. Follow me."

I'd only taken three steps into the room when a rustling sound had me turning my head. Edith stood at a desk, rifling through papers. She was muttering to herself as she flicked through the documents.

I tiptoed closer, Archie a breathy shadow behind me, meaning to ask Edith what she was doing. She should be selling brownies to the last of the festivalgoers, or packing away her stand, not looking at papers on Remus's desk.

"I knew it!" she murmured. "Remus did this."

My head tilted. "What did he do?"

Chapter 20
Secret identity

Edith jumped, her hand settling against her chest. "Oh! You scared me!" She shuffled papers back into a file.

I walked closer. "Sorry. Archie wanted to show off his new gift from Remus."

Her fingers fluttered in the air. "His portrait? That was nice of him. You're a sweet hound."

"Remus is always telling me that." Archie cocked his head. "What are you looking for?"

Edith hesitated. "I needed to check some paperwork."

I wandered to the sleepy vampires, still keeping an eye on Edith. Most vampires became lethargic during the day, unless they were particularly strong. These four had their eyes half-closed, satisfied smiles on their faces as they lounged.

I re-joined Archie and was about to jump on the desk, but Edith waggled a finger at me. "Better not risk it. A cat needs a tail for balance, and you don't want to hurt yourself by misjudging."

I recalled several recent clumsy attempts at jumping and remained where I was. "What are you still doing here? Everyone is leaving today."

"I was going today, too." Edith stepped around the desk and smoothed her hands down the front of her plain black outfit. "But then I got an offer I couldn't refuse."

Archie's ears pricked. "Someone just opened the fridge door. I'll be back in a minute." He bounded out of the room.

Edith chuckled. "That one is full of beans. I'll have to get used to all that energy, since I'll be seeing much more of him."

"Why is that?"

"Remus has just hired me. I'm joining the household as his part-time baker."

"That's an interesting career path." I glanced over my shoulder and saw empty plates covered in brownie crumbs beside the vampires. "Are these your test subjects?"

She smiled. "In a way. They persuaded me to make them something special. I haven't officially started yet, but I couldn't refuse their charm. Vampires can be so flattering."

"They look happy with whatever you gave them."

"I hope so. The undead are complicated when it comes to food, so I need to get the balance right. Still, I have plenty of time." She gestured at the desk. "I was just signing my contract and putting in an order for supplies."

A vampire tumbled off the couch, causing me to jump.

I hurried over to him. "Time for you to get to bed. You're too sun sensitive to be in here. You need a darkened room. Maybe Remus has one of those spare coffins lying around you could use."

"I'm good." He giggled as he tried to stand, but landed back on his hands and knees. "More brownies, please."

"I'll draw the curtains." Edith bustled to the window. "I'm not used to being around vampires, so I wasn't sure how to look after them. Should I have told him to go to bed and not fed him?"

"By the looks of this one, he's been partying too hard. He'll need a couple of days of rest, but he'll be fine once he's had a decent feed and some sleep." I nudged the vampire toward the couch to stop him from crawling closer to the windows.

Edith drew the curtains over two large windows, but left them open on the smaller window by the desk, so we weren't plunged into gloom.

"Maybe it's my fault he's so sluggish," she said. "I made my strongest batch of brownies to test on them. I said one each, but that greedy thing ate three, and there was nothing I could do to stop him."

"It's not your fault. Vampires often overindulge when they find something they enjoy," I said. "After all, they have no fear of making themselves unwell if they eat or drink too much. Not like me and you. We must know our limits."

Edith lifted her eyebrows. "I'd never thought about it until now. I suppose that's why so many people desire to be changed into a vampire. No consequences for your actions. It does sound tempting."

"It does. But we still need to be responsible for our behavior." Although, in my past, I'd not always owned up to everything I'd done, and that had caused chaos.

"I'll have to speak to Remus the next time I see him. Ask him to ensure his vampires don't overindulge on my treats, or I'll be baking non-stop and never have any rest," Edith said.

"You'll find Remus is a decent employer. He's generous with his vampires, so I'm certain he'll look after you." I gave up trying to get the vampire onto the couch and left him shuffling about on the floor. His three companions were giggling as he slid across the carpet. "Will you live in Crimson Cove?"

Edith collected her purse. "I'll have to see how busy Remus keeps me. If I'm only here for a couple of days a week, I can come and go as I like."

"Maybe he'll offer you a room. He has plenty that are empty."

"I hadn't considered that." She rested her purse over her arm. "At my age, I fear I'm too sedate for vampires. An early night and a warm mug of cocoa is about as exciting as I get."

"Whatever you decide, you'll be happy working for Remus. And my witch enjoys your brownies, so she'll stop by once you've settled in."

"I look forward to it." Edith smiled. "How did you like the wonderful portrait Remus commissioned for Archie?"

"It's one-of-a-kind. Remus is always treating Archie."

"It's extraordinary, isn't it? I made the treats. Remus requested them especially from me. I felt honored."

"The treat dispenser is a great feature." My stomach grumbled again. "Shall we take another look?"

Edith's gaze went to the door. "I should go. I have so much to do."

"Just for a minute. You can tell me more about the treats. They taste so good."

She indulged me with a smile. "Very well. But only for a few minutes."

We returned to the study and stood back to examine the portrait.

"They make a handsome pair," Edith said.

"Archie has been so happy since he joined with Remus. They're good for each other."

"A vampire and a hellhound. It's an odd combination." Edith tilted her head. "It's unfair they get a bad reputation, but seeing how Remus looks after his hive, it made me realize he's one of the good ones."

"His love for Archie proves that. They're practically inseparable. Well, until someone opens the fridge and the prospect of tasty food is presented to Archie."

Edith chuckled. "That hound has an appetite. I've had to refill the treat dispenser three times. You want to see the secret?"

"Of course!"

Edith shuffled behind the portrait and crouched. "The dispenser activates by sensor when Remus's hand is touched." She showed me how it worked and where the treats were contained. When she lifted the lid, a heady, meaty aroma hit my booping snooter.

"It's such an intense smell. I've tasted nothing quite like it."

"It's a secret recipe." Edith slid out from behind the portrait. "I'll be in charge of ensuring Archie's favorite treats are always stocked. Remus asked me not to spoil the illusion that it was a never-ending supply of delicious goodies, though."

"Archie won't mind if he learns the truth, just so long as he gets regular feeds."

"Oh, he will. He's always dabbing his nose on Remus's hand." Edith stepped back from the portrait. "I enjoy going to events, but as I get older, it gets wearing. It'll be nice to have a base and put down roots."

"And we're happy for you to make this your home," I said. "You'll find Crimson Cove welcoming."

"That's kind of you to say." She opened her purse. "I've been trying different flavors of treats. Archie seems most fond of the meaty variety."

"He's a sucker for a good hunk of steak," I said.

"Perhaps you'd like to sample the salmon? Made to my own unique recipe. Once you have one, you won't be able to resist more."

"Salmon! My favorite. I've not had much salmon recently. It's no longer on the menu in my favorite café."

"Of course. I visited there when I first arrived. I asked for an egg sandwich and was told they only sell plants."

"Blame the owner's new boyfriend. Your eggs are gone, and so is my salmon."

"Well, there's no reason to resist here. My treats are combined with fresh salmon and my unique flavor combination, then baked to perfection."

"Sounds idyllic. Sign me up."

"Give me a moment to put them in the dispenser. You wait by Remus's hand, and when I say go, press your nose on the portrait."

I was practically drooling as I waited for Edith to shuffle behind the portrait, but when I got my first whiff of intense salmon yumminess, I knew the wait would be worth it.

Edith appeared again. "Your treats are ready." She opened her purse and pulled out a small lunch box with a cut apple inside.

"No brownie for you?" I resisted the urge to indulge.

"I eat so many brownies when I'm working that I get sick of them. Besides, an apple a day keeps the doctor away. Go on, eat your treats."

I inhaled deeply and reverently pressed my booping snooter against Remus's hand. There was a faint click and a small door opened to reveal three dark brown treats. I sniffed them, then gobbled them down. I got an intense hint of salmon, a tangy twist of herbs, and something I couldn't identify.

"What do you think?" Edith bit into a piece of apple.

"Delicious. I can see why Remus hired you." I licked my lips.

"Go on, have more. I won't tell anyone."

"I shouldn't. They're for Archie."

"He prefers the meaty treats, so he won't mind. And that's what I'm here for. I feed the vampires and Archie whatever they desire."

What little willpower I had left vanished, and I dabbed my booping snooter against the portrait multiple times, gobbling down the treats that appeared.

"There's nothing better than good food with friends," Edith said.

I giggled as I overindulged. I should stop eating and find Archie. Or get back to Zandra and make sure she was okay. But the treats were so moreish, I couldn't stop. I gorged until my stomach bulged.

When I turned to look at Edith, she was staring at me with wide eyes. "Is something wrong? Sorry, I know I ate a lot."

"Extraordinary. You're still standing."

I hiccupped and then giggled again. "Why wouldn't I be? Although you'll have to roll me home if I take another bite of food."

Edith set down her purse. Her gaze went to the empty treat dispenser. "I've underestimated you. What kind of magical creature are you?"

I stared at her, unable to focus. Something felt wrong. My stomach churned. Bright dots of light danced in my vision, and my skin itched. I burped, then the room went black.

Chapter 21

Soiled salmon

A hot, raspy cloth was dragged repeatedly from my head down to my tail stump. A huff of meaty smelling air accompanied it.

Lick, rasp, huff. Lick, rasp, huff.

Then something cold dabbed my side, before the process began again.

I cracked open one eye just as Archie swiped his tongue over me.

He whined when he saw me awake and dabbed his nose against mine. "I couldn't get you to wake. When I found you on the floor, not moving, I thought you were dead!"

I groaned and tried to stand, but my stomach rolled over, so I remained on my side beside the portrait of Archie and Remus. "What's going on?"

"I don't know! I went to the kitchen to find out who opened the fridge door. Remus was in there, and he distracted me with leftover salami. When I came back, I found you like this."

My stomach continued to assault me, but I gently eased to my paws. My head pounded and my toe beans tingled. "Where's Edith?"

Archie whined. "Are you sure you're okay? Should I get Zandra?"

"She'll already know something is wrong with me. Edith was here. She was feeding me salmon treats from your portrait dispenser. Then she said something weird." I shook my head, regretting it as the pounding grew worse. "She said something like I was extraordinary."

"You are! You're the most extraordinary cat I've ever met. I'm proud to call you a friend."

"No, not that. She said something else. She said she'd underestimated me." I licked my lips and swallowed, the unpleasant aftertaste of the treats lodging in my throat. "I need some water."

"I'll get you my bowl." Archie bounded away, returning less than thirty seconds later with a metal water bowl in his mouth, slopping the contents across the floor. He set it in front of me and waited patiently as I drank my fill.

Only when the foul taste had left my mouth did I look up. "What did Edith mean?"

"I don't know. Who is she?"

"She was in here with the vampires." I glanced at the couch and chairs. The vampires were fast asleep. "Edith's been hired by Remus as his part-time baker. She's responsible for your treats in the dispenser."

"I know nothing about a new hire. I saw that old lady, but thought she was a cleaner. Remus has several women who clean for him. He always hires matronly types. Says they remind him of his mother, but I rarely see them because we're usually sleeping when they're here."

"Edith came here for the Blood Moon Festival. She said Remus was so impressed with her brownies that he hired her."

"He wouldn't do that. Remus is careful with who he brings into the household. If he's considering recruiting anyone, he interviews them three times, makes them stay overnight so they know what to expect when living in a vampire household, and then gives them a trial. That's only after collecting references. He'd never hire Edith on the spot."

I looked at the desk. "So, if she wasn't signing her contract and ordering supplies for her baking, what was she doing?"

Archie growled. "Was she snooping at something she shouldn't?"

"Juno! Where are you?" Zandra's voice carried along the corridor, the note of panic in it clear.

"In here," I called out pathetically.

She rushed through the door and scooped me up before I had a chance to tell her to be careful. She hugged me close. "What happened? It was like you vanished for a minute."

Now I was in my wonderful witch's arms, I instantly felt better. The sickness faded and I could think clearly. "I appear to have been drugged."

Zandra's eyes sparked with anger. "Who drugged you? Why?"

"It must have been Edith. She encouraged me to eat treats from the dispenser. She put in a special salmon flavored batch just for me."

"Edith?" Zandra said. "The lady selling those weird brownies?"

"Yes. I found her in here. She said she was ordering supplies for her new job working for Remus. I had no reason to think it was odd, but Archie told me Remus didn't hire her."

"He has protocols, and he checks with everyone to ensure we approve of any new recruits. Some people can be weird around vampires, so he's always careful," Archie said.

"We need to know what she was looking at. Take me to the desk." In my fragile state, I was happy for Zandra to carry me. Although with each passing minute, I felt less under the influence of Edith's devious treats.

Zandra's expression was tight with concern. "I should take you to the vet."

I hissed. "That's a terrible idea. I always come out feeling worse than I did when I went in. Let's figure out what Edith was up to. That'll make me feel better."

Archie joined us as we looked through the papers scattered across Remus's desk. "He didn't leave this mess. Remus is careful about tidying. He says everything has its place."

"These are files on his vampires," Zandra said. "I recognize some names and pictures."

"What's this open one?" I looked at the personnel file.

"Drayton Emory," Zandra said. "He's handsome. Exactly the type of vampire Remus likes to have around."

"Edith mentioned a son called Drayton," I said. "Could it be the same person?"

Zandra lifted the file so we could get a better look at the picture. She flicked through the pages. "This can't be her son. There's a note to say Drayton was turned into a vampire, but the turning failed."

"He's dead?" I said.

"In paradise," a drugged vampire slouched on the couch murmured.

"Paradise? What do you mean?" I asked.

He giggled.

"Take me to that vampire," I ordered Zandra.

"What's wrong with them?" She hurried over to the sleepy vampires with Archie dogging her heels.

"I fear they've had the same intoxicating substance as me," I said. "I found them in this state when I arrived, but I thought it was the effects of daylight making them drowsy."

Zandra nudged the woozy vampire with the toe of her boot. "Tell us about paradise."

The vampire's eyes were barely open, and his dark hair tumbled across his face. "They all go to paradise. It's a promise Remus makes to them."

"What is paradise?" I said.

The vampire chuckled. "Remus never kills those who fail in their turning. They're still part of this hive. Deadly members."

"You mean the feral spa? Remus told us about the secure place he sends vampires who can't control themselves."

The vampire nodded. "Remus is a good master. The best. Takes care of everyone."

"Is Drayton Emory a feral vampire?" Zandra said.

The vampire giggled. "I need more blood treats. Where's the brownie lady? She said she'd bring some back, but that was ages ago."

I drew in a breath. "We've just found out what happened to Briar's blood. She's been concealing it in her brownies and the treats she fed me and Archie."

Zandra poked out her tongue. "All of them? You mean, I could have been eating Briar? Gross!"

"It's not the first time we've come across blood brownies," I said. "It's a crafty way to hide the evidence. Gruesome, but clever."

"Need more brownies," the vampire muttered. "Delicious."

Archie whined. "I feel bad."

"You ate too many treats, just like me," I said. "Drink water. That helped settle my stomach."

"No! Not that kind of bad." He tipped back his head and howled, the tone ripping through me as echoes of misery vibrated around the room.

I struggled out of Zandra's arms and landed gently on the carpet. "Archie. What's the matter?"

His howl faded to a whimper as his body shook. "There's something wrong with Remus."

Chapter 22

Vampire stake

"How do you know Remus is in trouble?" I touched Archie's side to stop him from howling, since the sound curdled my insides and made my head hurt.

"We have a bond. It's like you and Zandra. We know when one of us is unhappy. This isn't unhappiness I'm feeling. It's... I don't know. Something wretched. It hurts."

"Is Remus in pain?" I said.

Archie whimpered, his sides heaving in and out. "I feel him, but he's weak and our bond is unstable. It may break at any second. He's in terrible trouble. I must find him."

"We'll help you look for Remus," Zandra said. "When was the last time you saw him?"

"In the kitchen."

"Remus could still be there," I said.

"No. He's been gone about fifteen minutes. Remus was feeding me and telling me what a good boy I was when he got a message. He didn't say what was in it, but he looked worried. When I asked him if I could help, he said it was personal business."

"Who was the message from?" Zandra was already heading to the door.

"I don't know. He left, I finished my snacks, and then came to find Juno. That's when I found her passed out. It took me ages to wake her."

The fact I was still soggy from head-to-tail stump and stank of Archie's drool revealed just how long he'd been licking me. "Edith must be behind all of this."

"You really think that old lady is a murderer?" Zandra reached the kitchen and pushed open the door. The room was empty.

Archie whined. "Hurry! Something bad is happening."

"We'll find Remus," I said. "Let's search the rooms. He'll be here somewhere."

We searched the mansion from top to bottom, but other than finding more drugged vampires, Remus wasn't inside.

Archie was panting as he raced around looking for Remus, his panic making him knock over furniture and slam into walls.

I hurried to him and rested a paw on his side. "Remus is a strong vampire. Even if he's in trouble, he'll get himself out of it."

"I've never felt this before," Archie said. "It's different. If our bond breaks, I'll break too."

"I'll check the basement. You two wait here." Zandra dashed down the wooden steps.

"Remus has too much to live for to get himself killed by an old lady wielding a pan of brownies." I said. "He'll fight. And when we find him, we'll help him if he needs it. Your vampire will soon be back by your side."

Archie hid his enormous nose under one paw. "Why is Edith doing this to us?"

"Because of someone she loves. Someone she thinks Remus wronged."

"Edith is here for revenge?"

I nodded.

"Remus isn't in the basement." Zandra returned from her search. "Loads of coffins, though. I checked them all."

"He must have gone outside," I said.

Archie whimpered. "Or been taken."

I stepped in front of my panicked friend. "I need you to focus."

"How can I focus when Remus is in trouble?"

"You must. Use that incredible nose to find him. I know you can do this. You know his scent better than anyone else."

Archie took a shuddering breath, then sniffed the air. "He's everywhere. All I can smell is him."

"Find the most recent scent trail," I said. "We'll follow that and it'll lead us to Remus."

It took Archie a few minutes to focus as he paced in a circle several times. Then his tail flicked, and he dashed toward the entrance hall. We ran after him. Archie charged out of the main door and into the cloudy afternoon, sniffing and snorting as he orientated himself to Remus's scent.

Dahlia and Primrose were loading their things into a cab, so I hurried over to them. "Have you seen Remus and Edith?"

"I saw Remus about ten minutes ago." Dahlia set her bag down. "And he was with an old lady. It was sweet. They were walking arm-in-arm."

"Did he seem okay?"

"He was staggering, but I figured that was because he was outside in daylight. Is something wrong?"

"Which way did they go?"

Dahlia pushed her glasses up her nose. "I'm not sure."

"They went to the woods," Primrose said. "I watched them."

"Is everything okay?" Dahlia said.

"It will be soon." I dashed back to Zandra and Archie. "Archie, focus on scent trails that lead toward the woods. Remus was seen going that way with Edith."

He hunkered down, sliding from side to side, his nostrils expanding and contracting. "Got it!" Then he was off again.

"What does Edith want with Remus?" Zandra said to me as we dashed after Archie toward the trees.

"Revenge. That paperwork on Remus's desk relates to her son, Drayton."

"The guy who failed to turn? She blames Remus for his death?"

Archie was so far ahead of us, I could barely see him, but he was heading to the woods, so we kept following. "She must have found out Drayton came to Remus to be turned."

"And been heartbroken when it failed."

"I don't think she knows the full story, though. Drayton isn't dead, since he's a feral vampire living at Remus's spa paradise."

"So, somehow, Edith discovered Drayton came here, vanished, and goes all eye-for-an-eye and plans on killing Remus? Where does Briar's death fit into this?"

"Kill Briar. Frame Remus to ruin him, and hope the Vampire Council take his fangs, so he's left with nothing. That's a fate worse than a stake through the heart."

"And she'll need him far away from any other vampires. Even a drugged hive is dangerous." Zandra wheezed out a breath. "How did Edith get him alone? Remus is always surrounded by vampires or with Archie."

"Archie got distracted by food. So did the vampires. Edith drugged them so they wouldn't worry about their master. She must have sent Remus the message, asking him to meet."

"Is Edith even capable of killing Remus, since her magic involves food?"

"If he's weak enough. Edith needs to know Drayton isn't dead, before she does something she can't come back from. Let's hurry!"

We sped up, and I kept sight of Archie's tail as he plunged through the trees. He was forced to slow as he entered an untamed area of the woods so we could catch up with him.

"He's definitely in here." Archie was panting as he continued to sniff. "But his movement pattern is odd. He's walking in a zigzag."

"Because he's been drugged," I said. "Edith must have fed Remus her special brownies."

"And she's brought him here to hurt him?" Archie growled. "I don't care if she's a sweet old lady. I'll destroy her."

"Let's hope Edith sees sense, so it doesn't come to that." I slowed. There were voices up ahead. "This way. Zandra, keep an eye on Archie."

She nodded, understanding what I meant. We couldn't have a giant, loyal hellhound lose control.

We pushed past bushes and rounded trees. The voices grew louder. One of them was Remus's, and he didn't sound good, his speech slow and slurred. We dashed past an enormous spruce and found them.

Edith stood over Remus, who lay on the ground. He had three wooden stakes sticking out of him. Fortunately, none had been plunged into his heart.

"Edith! Stop!" I hurried toward her. "I know why you're doing this, but you're making a mistake."

A thunderous snarl came from behind me, and I turned just as Zandra lunged at Archie and tackled him to the ground, magic spinning around them as they rolled together.

My heart was in my throat as my wonderful witch tackled him, but she swiftly got Archie under control and pinned him to the ground.

She lifted her chin at me. "Go! I've got this. I won't let him get loose. Save Remus!"

I hurried toward Edith and Remus. "Put the stake down. Remus isn't a killer."

Edith's face was flushed, her lips contorted. "Go away."

"You don't want to do this. You can't want more death on your hands."

"How are you still standing?" Edith's voice trembled, as did the stake she had raised in one fist.

"Because I'm a ridiculously powerful supernatural creature, as you must have realized when I didn't fall down dead from the drugged treats you tricked me into eating."

Edith's face was a mask of pain. "This is my business. I have to do this. Remus is a monster."

Remus rolled about on the ground. His eyes flickered, and although he opened his mouth, no words came out.

"I know you think Remus has done a terrible thing to your son, but you've got it wrong," I said.

"I know what he is! And I know exactly what Remus did. He has to pay." A sob tore from her lips. "My boy. My beautiful boy is gone."

Pounding footsteps grew closer, and Dahlia, Keanu, Trent, and eventually Primrose appeared.

"We thought you might need help." Dahlia's gaze went to Remus, and she gasped. "What are you doing?"

"Giving him what he deserves," Edith said. "And I don't care you're all here to see. That won't stop me."

"You won't do it," I said calmly.

"I will! Remus killed my son."

"You think he did. Which is why you murdered Briar and tried to frame Remus, didn't you?"

Dahlia reached for Primrose's hand and gripped it. "The brownie lady killed Briar? Why?"

"Revenge against Remus. It's one of the most basic motives for murder." I took a couple of steps closer to Edith, but she raised the stake, so I stopped.

"Don't come closer. Remus is weak. One more stake in the right place and that's it for him." Edith's breath wheezed out of her in ragged pants.

"I don't understand," Trent said. "What has this old lady got to do with Briar? How did they know each other?"

"They didn't. I suspect Briar was simply in the wrong place at the wrong time," I said.

Edith brushed away my comment with a hand. "Maybe so. But she was rude to me. And when I talked to her about my son, she dismissed me. When I found her alone, it wasn't a hard decision that she'd be Remus's victim."

Remus groaned and mumbled something incoherent.

"But she wasn't his victim," I said. "She was yours. You made it look like she'd been killed by a vampire, hoping Remus would be hauled before the Vampire Council and they'd take everything from him."

"I told you I had nothing to do with her death," Keanu muttered.

I slid him a glare. "You were creeping on her, though. You stalked Briar and pestered her. We had every right to suspect you. Just as we did Trent after their heated arguments."

Trent's eyes widened, but he said nothing.

"And the investigation wasn't helped when Dahlia made herself a suspect by hiding her alibi because she was ashamed of being involved with a vampire. And Primrose clearly had jealousy issues with Briar.

All the suspects made it hard to see what was really going on."

Primrose huffed out a breath and folded her arms over her chest.

"But we never looked at Edith. Not seriously," I said. "Why suspect the sweet, friendly magic brownie seller, who looked out for people of murder?"

Edith's knees wobbled, but she remained standing over Remus.

I desperately wanted to swish my tail, but settled for a whisker twitch. "So, Edith, tell us how you did it."

Chapter 23

Setup revealed

Edith looked around the group, her body trembling and her movements jerky. "It wasn't so difficult. When I heard about the event this disgusting vampire was holding, I knew it was a sign to act. I had to be here to get revenge for what happened to Drayton."

"Who's Drayton?" Dahlia said.

"Edith's son," I murmured. "Correct me if I'm wrong, but I believe Drayton came to Remus because he wanted to be turned into a vampire?"

Edith nodded. "I tried to persuade him otherwise. I said it was too dangerous. But he wanted more from life. More than I could offer him. I've always lived simply, pouring my magic into my food. Drayton found that boring."

"So, he came to Oak Park Ridge, and Remus agreed he'd be an ideal candidate for the hive," I said.

"Then Remus murdered him." Edith snarled and jabbed the stake lower. "Drayton came here, and I never heard from him again. He promised me after he'd turned and completed his training, we'd reunite. That was eighteen months ago. When I wrote to Remus asking for an update, he ignored my letters."

"I had to." Remus's speech was slow and indistinct.

"Be quiet!" Edith pointed the stake at his heart. "No more lies from you. I've seen how you and your vampires operate. It's all smooth words and a facade of civility, but take off the velvet jackets and fake kindness and you're monsters."

"Remus isn't quite the monster you imagine him to be," I said.

"What did you do to our sister?" Dahlia said to Edith. "Briar wasn't perfect, but she didn't deserve to die."

Edith sniffed. "I am sorry for your loss. I should have chosen someone who came here alone, but we bumped into each other and she made a snide comment. So, I gifted her a brownie. After that, she was easy to handle."

"You took her somewhere out of the way," I said. "Your tent? You said you had to set up at the edge of the woods because you got here late. But you didn't arrive late, did you?"

"No. I planned it that way. We went to my tent, and I told Briar to sleep it off."

"That's where you killed her," I said.

"No wonder we found no blood in the woods," Zandra said.

"My great grandfather ran a slaughterhouse. Unfortunately, I saw some of his practices, so I know how to drain a body and what veins to tap."

"And when we first met, you had a kind of brownie prong to spear the treats and give them to customers. It has two prongs on the end. Is that right?" I asked.

Edith sighed. "You're too observant for your own good. I used my brownie tool to make the holes. It wasn't easy, but I achieved what I had to."

Dahlia swayed on her feet, and Primrose had to help keep her upright.

"Which is why the holes in Briar's neck weren't neat," I said. "Once she was dead, you moved her to the woods?"

"It wasn't difficult. It was the reason I camped so close to the trees. And I know what happens at festivals. Young couples sneak off for secret rendezvous, so I knew she'd be discovered and then the vampires would get in trouble. And I'd seen Remus go inside on his own, so I knew he had no alibi."

"And here's a disturbing piece of this mystery. You used Briar's blood in your brownies and treats," I said. "It was a twisted way to hide the evidence."

"Please say that's not true," Primrose said. "I've been eating that old lady's brownies ever since I got here. And I bought a dozen for our road trip home."

"I used aqueous transmutation to turn the blood into powder so I could use it like powdered sugar. I dusted the brownies with it." Edith lowered her gaze for a second, but then stared at me, her expression defiant. "Those vampires are greedy, so it was easy to stuff blood powdered brownies into them. And they kept asking for more. They knew my secret, but they wouldn't tell, so long as I kept them full and happy."

"And drugged," I said. "That's what you did to the vampires."

"I had no choice. To get to Remus, I had to weaken his hive, or they'd come for me."

"They'll still come for you," I said. "Drugged brownies won't work forever."

"I'll tell them not to hurt you," Remus mumbled.

"I care nothing about that. I just needed time alone with Remus. Once I've punished him for what he did to Drayton, I don't care if I live or die. I have nothing left to live for." She lifted the stake, preparing to plunge it into Remus's heart.

"Wait! Drayton is alive. Well, technically undead, but he's still here," I said.

Edith snorted a humorless laugh. "I saw the paperwork. Remus failed to turn Drayton. Instead, he drained him and dumped his body. My son is gone."

"No! Things didn't go to plan during Drayton's turning, but Remus never gives up on his vampires, no matter how they behave."

"It's true," Remus murmured.

Edith's bottom lip trembled. "You're only saying this to stop me from staking you."

"Remus, tell Edith about your feral paradise. That's where Drayton lives now, isn't it?"

Remus's eyebrows rose, then he nodded. "I am sorry for ignoring your letters, but I never like to admit when my turnings aren't perfection."

"You ignored them because you're guilty of murder and you refused to face the consequences."

Edith pressed a foot on Remus's chest. "I don't trust you."

"Remus, talk faster. Your life depends on it," I said.

Remus blinked slowly, then drew in a deep breath. "I didn't kill him. Juno is correct. Drayton came to me to be turned, but things didn't go to plan."

Edith loomed over Remus. "Where is his body? The least I deserve is to give my son a funeral."

"He won't appreciate that, dear lady. Drayton is a vampire. A very much walking and talking vampire." Remus glanced at me. "Just with a few control issues."

Edith gulped and lowered the stake. "Don't play with me. Drayton is alive?"

"Well, I suppose, technically, he's one of the undead," I said.

"May I?" Remus gestured to the stake sticking out of his left shoulder. "It stings."

"No. Stay where you are and leave the stake alone." Edith swiped sweat off her forehead.

Remus grimaced, but didn't try to remove the stake. "Your son is a strong, intelligent young man. He flew through my aptitude tests and we all agreed he'd make an excellent addition to the hive."

"My boy can do anything he puts his mind to."

"I have no doubt about that. But at the turning ceremony, things went wrong. Drayton panicked, and he fought me when I bit him." Remus lifted a hand as Edith drew in a breath. "It happens. Primal instinct kicks in and rational thought gets cut off. I stopped immediately, but it was too late. He was changing. And when someone fights the change, it rarely ends in success."

"But... he is still Drayton? I can see him?" Edith's words wobbled out of her mouth. "I want to see him."

Remus hesitated. "He's a different version of the son you remember. Drayton lives by his baser instincts these days. You may not like what you see."

A tear trickled down Edith's wrinkled cheek. "Will he remember me?"

"Of course. He has his memories. But he asked that you didn't find out what happened to him. I believe he was ashamed. Drayton said you told him it was too dangerous to attempt and he should have listened to you."

A shaky sigh slid from Edith's mouth. "That boy never listened to reason."

"I've helped him in every way possible. He's comfortable, and he wants for nothing." Remus eased himself onto one elbow. "But he's unsafe to be around, which is why I sent him to my feral paradise. Or spa if you prefer. It's a delightful place if you desire only to hunt and feast."

"You see," I said. "Remus isn't a killer. He's good to his vampires, even the ones who turn out differently than expected."

Edith took a few steps back and dropped the stake. "I thought he murdered my son. I wanted to destroy him. It was the right thing to do."

"Murder is never the right option." Zandra still had hold of Archie under a powerful spell, but he was no longer fighting to get free, his attention solely on Remus.

"Take me to see my son," Edith said.

Remus winced. "Are you certain? You might find it distressing."

Edith grabbed the stake and bared her teeth. "Take me to him, or I'll know you're lying."

I hopped forward and placed my front paws on Remus's chest, certain Edith wouldn't hurt me or him. She was grieving and scared, but had killed Briar out of desperation and a broken heart, not because of a dark blood lust to destroy. "Remus, if you want to live, you'll let Edith have access to Drayton."

He sighed. "It hurts my vampiric spirit to show others my vampires who struggle. So many people judge difference in a harsh light."

Edith shook her head. "He'll still be perfect to me. I must see him."

I looked at Remus and nodded.

He inclined his head. "Very well. I'll take you to Drayton. But you must prepare yourself."

"I'll take my son in any form I find him. He'll always be my baby."

"You should see Drayton and reassure yourself your son is still with us," I said gently. "Then you need to have a conversation with Angel Force. Briar's murder cannot go unpunished."

Edith lowered her chin. "I'll accept my punishment. Now, take me to my son."

I stood with Zandra, Archie, and Remus outside his mansion the following evening as dusk drew in.

Remus was waving off Edith, a cheery smile on his face. Two angels accompanied Edith, and traveling beside her, in a reinforced metal cage, was her drugged, feral vampire son. Drayton was as vicious and out of control as you could imagine. A primitive force of destruction and rage, only caring about where his next meal came from. And he tried to bite anyone who got too close. Apart from one person. His mother.

"Edith will lose a finger if she keeps feeding him those brownies through the bars," Zandra murmured as the back of the van doors were shut, concealing the angels, Edith, and Drayton from view.

"They keep him calm," Remus said. "When the dust settles, I'll ask her for the recipe. I could feed it to the other feral vampires, see if it helps with their erratic moods."

"I think Edith is the calming factor in this equation," I said. "As soon as Drayton saw her, he stopped snarling. He curled into a ball and whimpered."

"It was a remarkable reunion," Remus said.

Zandra shook her head. "It was the weirdest family reunion I've ever seen."

The van drove away, leaving a peaceful stillness after the chaos of the Blood Moon festival and the murder investigation.

Primrose walked over with Dahlia. She was accompanied by Galahad, who had his arm around Dahlia's waist and adoration shining in his eyes.

This vampire was smitten by this delightfully bookish witch.

"Thanks for letting us stay another night," she said to Remus. She looked at me. "I'm still in shock, although I'm glad you figured out what happened to Briar."

"Yeah, thanks." Primrose stood apart from them, looking on enviously as Galahad tucked a strand of hair behind Dahlia's ear.

"It was the least I could do," Remus said. "Your family has been accidentally mixed up in my business. If I'd told Edith the truth about her son, none of this would have happened. I feel responsible."

"You kind of are," I said. "And there'll be other families wondering what happened to their relatives. The other ferals who turned out different. Do you keep it a secret from all of them?"

He ducked his head. "I do. But I've learned from this. I'll make amends to the families and inform them what happened."

"And arrange visits?"

Remus inhaled deeply. "Perhaps. One step at a time. Drayton may have been the exception."

"What'll happen to Edith?" Dahlia said.

"She'll be tried for murder and imprisoned," I said. "We all heard her confession."

"About that. I've spoken to the Vampire Council," Remus said. "Edith has asked to be turned so she can join Drayton in the feral paradise."

"You'd do that for her?" Zandra said. "After everything she put you and your hive through?"

"I consider it a small compensation to make. I should have been honest with Edith and told her about Drayton and his fractured turning."

"What about the murder charge?" Dahlia said. "She will be punished for what she did to Briar?"

"Yes. I have holding facilities for vampires who commit crimes. Edith will not be free to do as she likes. And she'll only get visiting privileges with Drayton when she has shown she can behave. Edith's terrible crime will not go unpunished."

"Well, it's a kind of happy ending," I said. "Edith can be reunited with her son and they can be together forever, savaging any unfortunate meals that pass their way once she's served her sentence."

"It's not so happy for Briar," Dahlia said. "We'll never get her back."

"Can I have her bedroom now?" Primrose said. "She always got the biggest room. It wasn't fair. Now she's gone, it's mine."

Dahlia glared at her spoiled sister. "We'll talk about that. But it's time you got a job and started contributing to the household before we make any changes."

Primrose's mouth dropped open. "What do you mean?"

"You need to pull your weight. You're not a child. I indulged you and Briar for too long, but things are changing. For all of us." She rested a hand against Galahad's chest.

Primrose grumbled to herself and turned her back on her sister.

"We'll leave you to it," Dahlia said, smiling at us all. "Thank you for getting to the truth."

Remus bowed, while the rest of us nodded goodbyes and wished them a safe journey home.

Dahlia walked away with Galahad, and Primrose tagged along behind.

Cythera flew down from the sky, swirled around our heads, and thudded to the ground, sending up a shower of dirt.

She stood and glared at Remus. "I hope you've learned your lesson after this mess."

"Fear not, fine angel. Juno and Zandra have suitably reprimanded me. I shall wear a sack cloth and ashes to punish myself. Perhaps a daily birch flogging would be suitable, too?"

She tutted. "A secret feral paradise full of out-of-control vampires. I can't tolerate such a thing."

"It's existed hundreds of years and there have never been any problems." The humor in Remus's gaze vanished. "They're my vampires, and my responsibility. I take the greatest care of them."

"You shouldn't have hidden this from me." Cythera jabbed a finger at him. "We will talk about this feral paradise some more."

"Shall I order a cream tea and we can converse in a civilized manner at your earliest convenience?"

Cythera turned away from him and stared in the direction the van had traveled, her shoulders tight and her arms folded.

"You seem angrier than usual," I said to her. "Is there anything we can assist with?"

She kept her gaze forward. "You've assisted enough. You should have called me in when you learned what was happening at Remus's mansion.

Instead, you raced around the woods acting like a superhero and saving the day."

"I never act," I said.

Cythera turned her head and glowered at me. "It isn't your responsibility to save everyone in Crimson Cove."

"Well, we're in Oak Park Ridge, so technically, I saved no one in our town."

"Don't be smart. It doesn't suit you." Cythera fluttered her wings behind her. "Things will move swiftly with Edith and Drayton. The Vampire Council has already spoken to me."

"We never like complicated issues to linger. And I'll be at Edith's disposal whenever the turning needs to take place." Remus bowed at the waist again.

While Cythera continued chastising Remus, I crept away with Zandra. We headed up the hill and stopped at the stone where I'd found more gremlin chaos symbols.

Zandra lifted me into her arms. "Another mystery solved. We found the killer. Edith will be reunited with her son, and Remus is in the clear."

"Not if Cythera has anything to do with it." I rested my paws over Zandra's shoulder. I could still hear Cythera's stinging tone.

"He shouldn't have kept the feral paradise a secret, but his heart was in the right place." She rested her hand on my tail stump. "Things feel different, though. We still have a few loose ends to tie up."

"My tail will return." I shifted in her arms.

"I'm sure it will. But it's not that. Something is stirring. And... you're different."

I tensed in her arms. "Different how?"

"It's been weeks since you gifted me anything dead."

I froze. I hadn't had a hunt urge for days. "I've been busy. A twisty murder mystery takes focus."

"You've solved mysteries before and still found time to drop disgusting dead things on my pillow." Zandra ran her fingers through my fur. "I'm not complaining, just pointing out the evidence that things are evolving."

"I'll make up for my lack of gifts. How about a squirrel?"

"No! I'm happy with this change. Thrilled. And sometimes, change is a good thing."

I huffed, annoyed with myself for failing in my duties. "These symbols aren't a good thing, though."

Zandra let out a gentle sigh. "Are they as problematic as you think they could be?"

I twisted my head and inspected the symbols. "I fear so. When we're ready, our next mystery awaits us."

Zandra kissed my head. "And together, we'll solve it."

I leaned into her cuddle. "We always do."

About Author

K.E. O'Connor (Karen) is a mystery author living in the beautiful British countryside. She loves all things mystery, animals, and cake.

If you want to practice spells, solve a few murders, and spend time with amazing witches and their talking familiars, join her weekly newsletter.

Sign up today.

Newsletter: https://BookHip.com/GXDVFRA
Website: www.keoconnor.com/writing
Facebook:
www.facebook.com/keoconnorauthor

Also By

Witch Haven: Welcome to Witch Haven, where nothing is what it seems. Meet four fabulous witches as they struggle with their destinies, deal with misfiring magic, murder, and the Magic Council.

Crypt Witches: Meet Tempest Crypt, a witch who swallows demons, and Wiggles, her mini talking hellhound, while you enjoy magical murder and intrigue.

Lorna Shadow: A cozy mystery series set in the fun world of a personal assistant who sees ghosts. Meet Lorna, her ditzy sidekick, Helen, and Flipper, the dog who senses ghosts, as they solve crimes and save the day.

Holly Holmes: An adorable cozy culinary mystery series set in the beautiful village of Audley St. Mary. Each book is full of treats, murder, and twists. Join Holly and Meatball, her clue-hunting dog, as they solve murders and eat cake.

www.ingramcontent.com/pod-product-compliance
Lightning Source LLC
Chambersburg PA
CBHW020748190726
48285CB00006B/1928